A novel based on the major motion picture

A novel based on the major motion picture

**Screenplay by Robert Rodriguez
Adapted by Kiki Thorpe**

talk miramax books
Hyperion Books for Children

New York

Text copyright © 2002 by Miramax Film Corp.

Story, art, and photographs
copyright © 2002 by Miramax Film Corp.

SPY KIDS™ is a trademark and the exclusive property of
Miramax Film Corp. under license from Dimension Films, a
division of Miramax Film Corp. All rights reserved.
All photographs by Rico Torres. All rights reserved.

No part of this book may be reproduced or transmitted in any
form or by any means, electronic or mechanical, including
photocopying, recording, or by any information storage and
retrieval system, without written permission from the publisher.
For information address Hyperion Paperbacks for Children,
114 Fifth Avenue, New York, New York 10011-5690.
ISBN 0-7868-1725-9
Printed in the United States of America
First Edition
1 3 5 7 9 10 8 6 4 2

If you purchased this book without a cover, you
should be aware that this book is stolen property.
It was reported as "unsold and destroyed" to the
publisher, and neither the author nor the publisher
has received any payment for this "stripped book."

Bright and early one Sunday morning, the Troublemaker Studios Theme Park was jam-packed with people. The members of the crowd peered over each other's heads, hoping to catch a glimpse of Alexandra, the eleven-year-old daughter of the president of the United States, who was visiting the park that day. Surrounded by a mob of Secret Service agents, Alexandra posed with theme park mascots, smiling cutely as tourists and photographers snapped her picture.

"We want to welcome our distinguished guest to our park here today—the president's daughter!" a theme park spokesman announced. The people in the crowd cheered and frantically clicked the shutters of their cameras. "Hello, Alexandra," the spokesman said, turning to her. "Where's your father?"

"Oh, my father will be here," Alexandra told him. "I'll make sure of that."

Just then, a goofy-looking man in a big cowboy hat and a funky Western jacket stepped over to them. It was Dinky Winks, the theme park engineer. Dinky had designed nearly every ride in the theme park, and he wasn't about to miss the chance to show off his work. He flashed a white-toothed grin at Alexandra.

"Ready to ride the rides and shrill to the thrills, little lady?" he bellowed in a Texas accent.

"Yes, I am," Alexandra replied.

"Then skidoodle over this way." Taking her elbow, Dinky steered the president's daughter toward the park's greatest attractions. "Of course, we got the world-famous Whippersnapper over there," he said, pointing to a ridiculous-looking ride whipping people through the air nearby. "Guaranteed to make a grown man cry for momma," Dinky added proudly.

Alexandra glanced at the ride and yawned. Dinky frowned. It seemed Alexandra was a tough customer. He was going to have to up the ante.

"Over to your left . . ." he began. Alexandra looked to the right. Dinky followed her gaze to a jittery-looking ride. "The NerveWracker," he explained. "Painful and fun. Over to your *other* left is my personal favorite," he continued, steering Alexandra toward the ride on their left. The ride was spinning so quickly that all they could see was a blur of movement. "The Vomiter," Dinky told Alexandra. "We tell people not to ride with a full stomach. But you know how it is. They just don't listen." Dinky suddenly opened a clear umbrella, just in time to shield them from the spray of vomit that flew from the ride.

"But why bother with any of those?" Dinky said, spinning on his heel to face Alexandra. "Sure, they're tried-and-true. But you're here for my latest and greatest. . . ." Dinky waved dramatically toward the ride: "The Juggler."

The Juggler towered over them. High above the ground, the ride's compartments spun through the air, unattached by bars or cables. Dinky's face glowed with pride as he watched it. It was indeed a feat of engineering genius.

"But is it fast?" asked Alexandra.

Dinky chuckled. "Let's see, shall we?" he said. He summoned two parents and their children over to test the ride. "The riders are strapped into the Bubble," Dinky explained to Alexandra as the family climbed aboard the ride. "The Bubble spins, flips, turns, and bounces."

Looks of panic crossed the test family's faces as their Bubble bobbled wildly.

As the ride lifted off the ground, Dinky continued to narrate. "The Hydrobot lifts the Bubble high into the air. Spins it around and around, as fast as the United States government will allow. Then . . ."

Watching the ride, Alexandra's eyes lit up with excitement. "It *juggles* you," she said breathlessly. Dinky winked.

"I want to go on," Alexandra said.

Dinky nodded. "I thought so. Understand, the override precautions are top-notch, modified by yours truly, and safer than a dead polecat." He showed Alexandra a hidden panel of blinking buttons. Alexandra looked at them thoughtfully.

Dinky leaned over to a nearby Secret Service agent. "I thought her father was supposed to be here," he whispered.

"He had more pressing business than to spend a whole Sunday at a theme park," the agent explained.

Dinky frowned. "No one's that busy," he said. He glanced sympathetically at the young girl.

Little did he know that behind his back, Alexandra was sneakily shutting down the ride's safety override. She pulled the control key from the panel of blinking buttons and stuck it in her pocket. Then she turned to Dinky.

"I'm ready," she said.

Dinky escorted her to the ride and helped her buckle her seat belt.

"Have fun, kid. Enjoy," he said, as he shut the door to her Bubble.

As Alexandra's Bubble started to spin, a girl and boy stepped forward to get a better view. They both wore Troublemaker hats, but they weren't your average tourists. They were Carmen and Juni Cortez, agents in an international network of spies! And today they were on special assignment.

Carmen rolled her eyes as she watched Alexandra. "She wants to ride the Juggler. Meanwhile, we're stuck baby-sitting," she muttered.

"It's not that bad," Juni replied, his eyes locked on Alexandra.

Carmen looked at her younger brother. "You just have a crush on her," she said.

"Well . . ." Juni blushed. After all, the president's daughter was awfully pretty.

Carmen shook her head. "Stay away from her," she warned. "She's bad politics."

The Bubble carrying Alexandra lifted into the air. At the ride's control, Dinky told the operator, "We'll take it a little slower. Just make it fun."

But when her Bubble reached the highest point, Alexandra suddenly jammed her seat belt, stopping the ride just long enough for her to climb out onto the top of the mechanical arms. Standing at the top of the ride, she peered down at the crowd of people five stories below.

The crowd panicked. Tourists shrieked and pointed while park officials ran this way and that, trying to figure out how to get the president's daughter down from the ride. Meanwhile, the Juggler began to toss the giant bubbles through the air around her.

"Can't you shut it down?" the Secret Service agent screamed at Dinky.

"I'm trying!" Dinky cried. "Someone's jammed the override!" Just then he noticed that the key was missing from the control box. And he knew just who had taken it.

The head Secret Service agent stepped forward and flashed his badge. "Remain calm," he said. "We are the Secret Service. Everything is under control."

But everything was not under control. Just then, another Secret Service agent hurried over. "There's nothing we can do, sir," he told the head agent. "The weight of our agents will prevent us from ascending the shaky place on which she now stands. She'll fall if we go up."

"Don't we have any smaller agents?" the head agent exclaimed. The two men blinked as they suddenly realized they *did* have smaller agents. "Bring me SK1 and SK2," he ordered.

The Secret Service agent found Carmen and Juni eating cotton candy. But when Juni saw the president's daughter stranded atop the wild ride, he dropped his snack. "I'm ready," he said bravely.

"Use this. It's the latest gear," the agent said. He ripped the price tags off two new gadgets and handed them to Carmen and Juni.

Carmen carefully examined the gadget. "We get to keep them afterward?" she asked.

"Of course," said the agent.

Juni strapped the gear to his wrist. When he opened his hand, tiny grabbers fanned out like a deck of cards. He wiggled his fingers. "And you're sure these are the *latest* latest gadgets?"

"Are you kidding? Check out the metal . . . it's still molten. Hot off the production line," the agent assured them.

Satisfied, Carmen and Juni began to scale the Juggler. Using the tiny grabbers to cling to the metal structure, they pulled themselves up the side of the ride like a pair of spiders.

As they climbed, Carmen formulated their plan of action. "You grab her while I disengage the ride by accessing its mainframe." Juni nodded in agreement.

On the ground, the two agents watched them. "You sure they can handle this?" the head agent asked.

"If not, there are two others who can," the agent replied. He lifted his walkie-talkie to his lips. "Bring me agents SK3 and SK4," he commanded.

CHAPTER 2

Carmen and Juni were halfway up the side of the ride when they saw two new kids sprinting toward the Juggler. "We've got company," said Juni.

Juni used his bino-watch to identify them. Beneath computerized images of a boy and a girl, the watch screen displayed their data:

Gary Giggles: Age 15
Gerti Giggles: Age 10

"What are they doing here?" Juni groaned. He began to scramble double time. Carmen climbed faster, too. They weren't going to let the Giggleses take over their assignment.

Suddenly, six thin wires shot past Juni and attached to the ride frame above. Juni looked over and saw Gary Giggles sprinting past him— vertically!

"Excuse me there, sport," Gary said. He easily passed Juni, pulled upward by the wires.

Juni had never seen a gadget like that before. "Where did you get that?" he asked.

"It's the latest in electro-riser technology, with new composite materials and A.I. brainology." Gary smiled at Juni's baffled expression. "I can see you don't know what I'm talking about," he said smugly.

Juni frowned. "Gary, this is *my* rescue!" he told the older boy.

Gary smirked again. "We'll take it from here," he said. He flew up the wires, leaving Juni in the dust.

Juni climbed furiously, but his metal fingers were no match for Gary's fancy gadget. "Latest gear, my butt," he grumbled.

At the top of the ride, Gary had to cling to the shaking frame to keep from tumbling over the edge. He held out one hand toward the president's daughter. "I'll have you back down in a microsecond," he told her. But to his surprise, Alexandra pulled away.

"Get away from me!" she snapped. Just then Juni scrambled up the other side. "Alexandra, take my hand," he called.

"You, too! Back off!" she shouted at Juni.

Meanwhile, the Juggler juggled its bubbles around them faster and faster. The ride swayed beneath their feet. At any moment one of them could fall!

"I want my *father* to come up here and get me," Alexandra demanded.

"But he's the president of the United States," Juni said.

"No," Alexandra said firmly. "He's my *father*. He was my father before he was ever president, and he should still be my father now. I want *him* up here."

Far below on the ground, another Secret Service agent ran up to the agent in command. "Sir, we have a situation," he said. He whispered into the head agent's ear as a small fleet of black Secret Service cars pulled up, surrounding the entire area.

The head agent looked at him with alarm. "This is now a code red situation. Get her down *NOW*!" he commanded.

Back up on the ride, Juni tried to reason with Alexandra. "Don't be afraid," he told her.

"I'm not," she said.

"Maybe not of this," Juni told her. "But I know things haven't been cool between your mom and dad lately."

"How do you know that?" she asked, startled.

Juni lifted the badge that hung around his neck. "I'm a secret agent in the OSS," he explained. "We have access to that sort of information. The point is, you and your father need to talk. And up here may not be the best place." He held out his hand again to her. "Come with me. And I promise . . . the two of you will have that talk."

Alexandra's eyes narrowed suspiciously. "How can you promise that?" she asked.

Juni tapped his badge. "I'm Level Two," he told her. "I can *order* him to talk to you."

Alexandra looked at him in surprise—this kid could tell the president what to do?

Meanwhile, Gary glared enviously at Juni over the top of his sunglasses. He was only a Level Three spy, and he resented the fact that Juni had already made it to Level Two.

Down below at the ride's main control box, Carmen was working quickly to make the Juggler stop. As she yanked at a tangle of wires, Gerti Giggles popped up next to her.

"Whatcha doin'?" Gerti asked.

"Hi, Gerti," Carmen said. "I'm trying to stop the ride."

"Without disengaging the axis?" asked Gerti.

"Exactly," Carmen said as she pulled at another wire.

"Then stop what you're doing," Gerti ordered. Carmen stopped and looked at her in surprise. She watched, dumbfounded, as the younger girl pulled out a gadget and strapped goggles to her head. The gadget created a holographic template, which Gerti placed over the control box.

"The ride is designed to work like a giant magnet," Gerti explained. "If you reverse the polarization . . . bye-bye, president's daughter." Reaching into a pocket, she pulled out a pair of tweezers and nonchalantly plucked a hair from one of her eyebrows. Then she reached past Carmen and used the tweezers to pull one tiny switch. The ride slowed to a stop.

Gerti briskly packed up her gadget and dusted off her hands. "See ya around," she said pertly. She scooted back to the ground on her high-tech wires. Carmen furiously gathered up her tools and slammed the control box shut. She'd been outspied—and by a ten-year-old!

Up at the top of the ride, Juni sighed with relief as the ride stopped moving. The president's daughter caught his hand and he pulled her to safety. But just as he was about to take her down to the ground, Alexandra said, "Wait." She held up a small slab of silver metal with a red button in the center. "I took this from my father's office this morning," she told Juni. "I'm sure he'll want it back." She looked down at the ground, where ten more Secret Service cars had just pulled up. "It's probably why all those agents are showing up," she added.

Gary's eyes widened. He grabbed the device out of Alexandra's hand, nearly knocking Juni and Alexandra off the ride.

"Careful!" Juni cried.

"Look, Cortez," said Gary, pocketing the metal device. "You take *her* down, and I'll take *this* down. Then we'll *both* look good."

Juni glared at him. "I'm not doing this for looks, *Gary*," he said. He secured a cable to the metal framework of the ride. Then he punched in a code that would take them to the ground. Holding Alexandra, Juni leaped over the side of the Bubble. As they reached the ground, the cable slowed their fall, and they landed softly on their feet. Above, Gary clipped onto Juni's line and followed them down.

The instant Alexandra touched the ground, Dinky ran over and placed a Troublemaker hat on her head.

"Thanks for visiting—come back soon!" he cried, before the Secret Service agents escorted him away.

The agents quickly surrounded Alexandra. "Thank goodness you're all right," they said, patting her down as if she were an armed criminal. "We were worried sick that—"

"Oh, boys," Gary called. He waved the little metal device in the air. "I think *this* is what you're looking for."

"The Transmooker device!" The agents dropped Alexandra and rushed over to Gary.

"She swiped it from the president," Gary told them.

Two agents marched over to Alexandra and grabbed her arms. They began to haul her over to a waiting car. "You're in big trouble this time, missy," said one agent.

"Wait a minute!" Juni cried. "I promised her she could talk to her father."

"Oh, she'll be talking to him all right, squirt, " the agent said, brushing past Juni and throwing

Alexandra into the backseat of the vehicle. "We'll make sure of that." Alexandra threw a desperate look at Juni. Then the door slammed and the car sped off.

Juni watched as the Secret Service agents patted Gary's shoulders, congratulating him on his heroic deed. They packed the Transmooker device into a metal suitcase and placed it on an official helicopter. Gary grinned at Juni as he stepped into a cool-looking chopper car.

As the chopper car rose into the air, Carmen made her way over to Juni. "Promise me one thing," she said.

"What?" asked Juni.

Carmen glared after the chopper car. "No more Mickey Mouse assignments."

CHAPTER 3

"The Ukata assignment?" asked Carmen's mother, Ingrid, looking at her daughter in surprise. Then she shook her head. "Your duties are assigned to you by the agency, same as me."

It was the night of the OSS awards banquet. Ingrid sat at her vanity table with an array of colorful cosmetics spread out before her. She reached out and began typing on a palette of eye shadow. Suddenly, a message blipped up on the computer screen in front of her. The makeup was actually the keyboard of her secret spy computer!

Carmen stood next to her mother, trying on lipstick.

"Mom, we've learned so much already. Juni and I are *more* than capable of bigger missions," Carmen said.

Ingrid pursed her lips. "The Spy Kids organization is still new," she said. "If you're a Level Three or even a Level Two, you can't go on missions alone. You're agents in *training*." As a top-level spy herself, Ingrid knew how dangerous spy work could be. She looked back at the screen and punched a few more keys, signaling that their conversation was over.

Carmen sighed and looked over her mother's shoulder at the screen. "If you're looking for top-secret information, go straight to the source, Mom," she said. She leaned over and typed out a code on a few keys shaped like eye shadows. Suddenly an official-looking logo appeared on the screen.

"*Welcome to the Pentagon*," said a computerized voice.

"How did you do that?" Ingrid exclaimed. "You can't do that. No hacking in this household."

"I know. I'm sorry," said Carmen. She hit a few more keys and the logo disappeared.

Ingrid frowned. She looked at the computer screen. Then she looked back at Carmen. "Show me that again," she said.

A few rooms over, Juni and Gregorio Cortez, dressed in matching tuxedos, were combing their hair. That is, Gregorio was combing their hair.

"I know this hair thing is one of my weak-nesses," he said, dragging a metal comb through

Juni's curls. "You're looking cool, like *me*." Juni winced, fearing for his hair.

"That's my boy," Gregorio continued. He yanked the comb through a snarl. "Uh-oh. A knot. Hold on a second." Juni squirmed in discomfort. At this rate, he wasn't going to have any hair left!

"Last touch," said Gregorio, shoving Juni's hair up and forward so that he looked like James Dean. Juni looked unhappily at his hairdo.

"I think I'll get some hair glue from Mom," he said. "Should I wear a bow tie or a straight tie?"

"A bow is more appropriate. You want me to tie it for you?" asked Gregorio.

Juni shook his head. "RALPH can do it," he said. At Juni's command, RALPH, a small, spiderlike robot, crawled up Juni's arm and whipped his tie into a bow. When it had finished, Juni held out his hand. RALPH leaped off his shoulder, retracted its legs and head, and fell into Juni's palm like a small hockey puck.

Gregorio raised his eyebrows. "Interesting," he said. "But it can never replace me." He straightened Juni's tie so it was perfect.

"Not yet," said Juni. "But I think that new upgrade comes in next week."

Gregorio frowned. Juni grinned. "Only joking," he said.

As the Cortezes walked toward the OSS awards banquet later that evening, Ingrid pulled Carmen and Juni aside. "Now remember, kids," she told them. "This is a big night for your father. If he's named head of the OSS, be sure and stand up and give him a big hug."

"What if he doesn't win?" asked Carmen.

"Give him a bigger hug," Ingrid told her.

Inside a round, open-air room, spies wearing tuxedos and fancy dresses stood in groups chatting with one another. Waiters circled the banquet hall, offering trays of hors d'oeuvres and champagne. It looked like any other formal affair, except for one thing—half the people in the room were kids! A large banner over the door read OSS WELCOMES SPY KIDS FROM AROUND THE WORLD.

Carmen and Juni chatted in Mandarin with a pair of Spy Kids from China. As Carmen introduced the Chinese Spy Kids to some Spy Kids from France, a waiter came over to them. He held out a tray filled with glasses of champagne.

The kids looked at him in surprise. "We can't have any of that," Juni told the waiter. The waiter muttered an apology and slipped off to the next group. Juni watched him go, frowning. "Something doesn't feel right," he said to himself.

But just then Gary and Gerti Giggles walked through the door. "No wonder," Juni said. He nudged Carmen. "Your buddy is here," he said, pointing to Gary.

"He's not my buddy," Carmen told him.

"Your buddy with the weird laugh," Juni added.

"He does not have a weird laugh," Carmen snapped. She motioned Juni to be quiet as Gary and Gerti approached them.

"We were just talking about you," said Gerti.

"Really?" said Carmen. She turned to Gary.

"Heh, heh, heh," Gary chuckled.

Carmen drew back in surprise. Juni was right—Gary's laugh *was* creepy.

Juni smiled.

"Looking good, Carmen," said Gary. "Wanna dance?"

"Well . . ." Carmen glanced around to see if her parents were nearby. "Sure," she said.

But Juni stepped between them. "I don't think

that's a good idea," he said. "Family rules say you need to ask my father's permission."

Gary glanced at Juni as if he were a squashed bug. "You should have gotten that suit tailored," he said. "It's bunching up around your gut, and it makes your head look way too big."

Juni balled his fists, ready to strike. But Carmen stepped between them and pulled Gary aside. "You've got to forgive my little brother," she said. "He's still upset about the amusement park."

"A good agent controls his temper," Gary told her.

"Just be glad my dad isn't here," Carmen replied. "He's *really* wacko when it comes to—"

Whoops! Carmen turned and broke off suddenly. Her father was standing right behind her! He folded his arms and fixed them with a stern look.

"Hi, Dad," Carmen said brightly. "You remember Gary. He's in our organization."

"I was just asking your daughter for a dance," Gary said.

Gregorio raised his eyebrows. "Do you know how to dance?"

Gary nodded. "Fairly well, sir."

"What about the tango?" asked Gregorio.

"Yes," Gary answered.

"Rumba?"

"Mmm-hmm."

"Cha-cha?"

"Yes, sir."

"Pasa doble?"

"A few steps."

"Merengue?"

"The second half of that."

Gregorio smiled and glanced at Juni. "What about a waltz?" he asked Gary.

"Uh, yeah," Gary said hesitatingly. "I'm pretty sure I know that."

"Show me," Gregorio said.

Gary and Carmen began to dance around in a stiff, awkward waltz. As soon as their backs were turned, Gregorio and Juni looked at each other and burst out laughing. But the moment Gary turned around, they looked serious again.

"Okay," said Gregorio. "You can go dance." He smiled at Juni. "Look after your sister," he told him.

Juni smiled back and nodded. He followed Carmen and Gary over to the dance floor.

Just then Juni noticed a group of Secret Service agents dancing in a bunch. Peering in between their arms, he caught a glimpse of the president's daughter.

"What are you doing in there?" he called through a gap between the agents' elbows.

"Dancing," Alexandra replied.

"You always carry this many Secret Service agents around?"

"It's my dad's idea. He's gotten a little paranoid," Alexandra explained.

"Will you dance with me?' Juni asked. He bobbed up and down, trying to see between the dancing agents.

"No," said Alexandra.

Juni pulled out his badge and flashed it at the Secret Service men. "Level Two. Break it up." The cluster of agents split apart. There stood Alexandra in a fancy ball gown. To Juni she looked like a princess. A beautiful princess. They stood face-to-face, looking at each other.

"Why not?" he asked her.

"I only dance ballet."

Juni smiled. "What an incredible coincidence." He lifted his arms above his head and pointed his toes, striking a perfect ballet pose. "So do I."

"Are you serious?" said Alexandra.

Whoosh! To Alexandra's astonishment, Juni swept her off her feet. Together they danced a beautiful duet. Juni lifted her and dipped her as gracefully as a professional dancer.

Meanwhile, Gregorio was chatting with Gary and Gerti's father, Agent Donnagon Giggles. Donnagon was Gregorio's competition for the head of the OSS.

"May the best man win," said Gregorio.

"Thank you. I think I will," Donnagon replied.

Gregorio raised one eyebrow. "Confident? Or inside information?"

Donnagon scowled. "We could settle this the old-fashioned way," he growled.

Back on the dance floor, many couples had stepped aside to watch Juni and Alexandra. "I must say, you're a man of many talents," Alexandra said as Juni lifted her gracefully off the ground.

Juni shrugged modestly. "One tries," he said.

Nearby Carmen and Gary were still struggling through their waltz. "I'd say after a few more missions, I'll be ready to join the big leagues," Gary told Carmen.

"I guess that's a good plan," Carmen said. "To hit the top. Be number one."

Gary nodded. "A good spy always has his eye on the prize." Just then they noticed Juni dancing with the president's daughter. They quit waltzing and began to bust some hip-hop moves.

Ingrid saw them and smiled. She turned to Gregorio. "Care to dance?" she asked.

"Well, I . . ." Gregorio stuttered.

"Thought so," said Ingrid, yanking him to the dance floor. But it had been some time since they had danced together. When Gregorio tried to dip Ingrid, he lost his grip, and she hit the floor with a *thud*. Ingrid glared at him.

Clink, clink, clink! Suddenly a bell-like tinkle echoed through the room. Everywhere in the room, OSS agents jumped into defensive stances, ready to fight.

Felix Gumm, a member of the OSS, looked around the room in surprise. He was only tapping his champagne glass to get their attention. "Could everyone please take a seat?" he asked. The agents relaxed and moved over to the tables.

"I must go," Alexandra told Juni, as the Secret Service agents swarmed over and hustled her away. Juni's face fell—they'd only just started talking! As he walked to the table where his parents and

Carmen were seated, Juni noticed that Gary and Gerti Giggles were being escorted to a table right at the front of the room.

"Ladies and gentlemen . . . the president of the United States," a voice announced. The president stepped up to the podium. Someone brought out a TelePrompTer and placed it in his line of view. The crowd quieted.

"I am proud of the OSS and their newly formed Spy Kids division for their outstanding accomplishments yesterday," the president said stiffly, reading from the TelePrompTer. "Gary and Gerti Giggles not only *saved* my daughter . . ."

"What's he talking about? *I* saved her. . . ." Juni rose angrily to his feet, but Carmen pulled him back to his seat.

"But as important, if not *more* important," the president continued, "they safely retrieved the Transmooker device that my daughter accidentally took from my office earlier that day." He held up the little slab of metal with the red button. All the agents in the room turned and glared at Alexandra. She shrank back in her chair and looked over at Juni. He gave her a sympathetic smile.

"I would now like to announce our new head of

the OSS," the president said.

Gregorio sat up excitedly. Ingrid put her hand on his. Carmen winked at him from her seat.

"Gregorio . . ." the president said, looking at the TelePrompTer. Gregorio's eyes widened. Ingrid, Carmen, and Juni opened their mouths to cheer.

But suddenly the name on the TelePrompTer vanished and was replaced by a new one. "Oh, I'm sorry," the president said. "Donnagon Giggles!"

Gregorio's face fell. As the crowd cheered, Donnagon slapped high fives with Gary and Gerti, then stepped up to the podium. "Gary and Gerti Giggles are the kind of agents we need to turn the OSS around, making this agency an organization that once again instills *trust*," he said.

Around the room, agents at the tables nodded in agreement. The last head of the OSS had turned the spies against one another and used the organization for his own greedy purposes. Carmen, Juni, and their parents had helped put a stop to his evildoing. But as Donnagon went on, it became clear he wasn't thinking of the Cortez family at all.

"I'm proud to award Gary and Gerti these Level *One* badges," Donnagon announced, "which allow them to take on real missions. Something challenging like ... *the Ukata assignment*!"

Excited murmurs filled the room. For weeks everyone in the OSS had been talking about this mysterious assignment. Gary and Gerti leaped from their seats and stormed up to the podium, grinning like game show contestants.

"That's so unfair!" Carmen fumed, rising to her feet. "I wanted that assignment." Juni pulled her down.

"Now, kids," Donnagon said. "This mission is dangerous, difficult . . . some would even say *impossible*. Gary and Gerti, will you accept this honor?"

Gary and Gerti turned and faced their audience. "Yes, we will," Gerti said bravely.

Donnagon beamed. "I am proud to claim them as our organization's top Spy Kid operatives," he announced. "And I'm also proud to claim them ... of course ... as my children."

Whistles and applause filled the room. But the Cortezes weren't clapping. Carmen huffed and threw her napkin down in frustration.

"I don't know about this," Ingrid said.

Gregorio eyed Donnagon suspiciously. "This is all wrong," he agreed.

At the front of the room, Donnagon raised his glass for a toast. "To our Spy Kids!" Donnagon exclaimed.

"To our Spy Kids," the adult agents cheered. Together they lifted their glasses of champagne and drank.

A second later the glasses fell from their hands as they passed out cold at the tables.

CHAPTER 4

Carmen and Juni leaped to their feet. So did all the other Spy Kids. They were the only ones left standing!

Carmen sniffed the champagne glasses Ingrid and Gregorio had sipped from. "Sleepers!" she cried. Someone had drugged the champagne! But who?

Suddenly, all the waiters in the room dropped their trays and ran toward the president, who had passed out on the ground next to the podium. Juni jumped onto the table. "They're after the Transmooker device!" he shouted.

The Spy Kids sprang into action. Several agents raced to the doors and sealed off all the exits in the room. The other kids leaped onto their tables. Working in groups, they pounced onto waiters twice their size, dragging them to the ground. They used cords from the curtains to tie the waiters' hands and feet. Then they tied all the waiters together. A group of kids clung to one end of the cord and jumped from a second-floor balcony, using their weight to haul the waiters into the air. The waiters dangled in a clump above the room.

But they hadn't managed to catch them all. One waiter had reached the podium and grabbed the Transmooker device from the president's hand. Juni and Gary cornered him. "Outta my way, shorty," the waiter growled at Juni.

Juni hit a button attached to his suit. Suddenly his shoes sprouted springs. Juni shot three feet into the air. Now he was taller than the waiter!

"Who you calling 'shorty,' shorty?" said Juni. He reached out to slap off the man's hat. *Clang!* His hand struck metal! As Juni clutched his stinging fingers, the waiter kicked the springs out from under his feet. Juni crashed to the ground.

Gary leaped over Juni and tackled the waiter. The man threw him off as easily as a dog shaking off a fly. But Gary landed on his hovershoes. He zoomed back at the waiter, full speed, and knocked him off his feet. Juni saw his chance. He dove in and snatched the Transmooker device out of the man's hand.

Gary saw him. He forgot about the waiter, and grabbed the device away from Juni.

"Give that back!" Juni cried. He reached for Gary, and the two boys tumbled onto the ground, punching and kicking. They were so busy fighting, they didn't even notice the Transmooker device roll away.

The waiter grabbed it. As he turned to flee, a roomful of Spy Kids menacingly stepped toward him, brandishing dozens of different kinds of gadgets.

But the waiter didn't flinch. He raised the Transmooker device and aimed it at the kids' gadgets. When he pressed the button, all the gadgets fell to the ground, useless!

A row of kids crept up behind the waiter, but he spun around and fired the Transmooker device at them. All their gadgets failed, too! The Transmooker device rendered every gadget powerless!

Thinking fast, Carmen grabbed some spoons off a nearby table. Quick as lightning, Carmen flung the spoons at the waiter. *Whack!* They smacked him square in the forehead.

"Owww!" the man cried.

Carmen reached for more spoons, but suddenly the room began to shake. Carmen looked at the man—he was shaking, too! He smiled and stepped into the center of the room.

As he did, the spoons in Carmen's hand began to shake. She quickly let go and ... they floated into the air! Carmen stared. Suddenly, everything metal in the room flew upward. The kids looked up. A strange aircraft was hovering above them, and all the metal objects were stuck to the bottom of it. The ship was some kind of magnet! The waiters shot off the ground, attaching to the bottom of the ship by their metal hats.

At that moment, the adults opened their eyes. Everyone watched in astonishment as the ship flew away into the night with the waiters dangling from the bottom. Everyone, that is, except Juni and Gary. They were still wrestling on the floor.

Carmen rushed to break them apart. "Get off him, Juni!" she cried, pulling her brother up. Juni stood in his rumpled tuxedo, glaring at his sister. She was standing next to Gary, and to Juni it looked like she was taking Gary's side.

Suddenly, the president cried out, "They got away with the Transmooker device!"

Everyone turned to look at Juni. Juni looked around the room, hoping someone had seen what had happened. But each face glared at him accusingly. Even his own parents looked uncertain. At last he saw Alexandra. Just as their eyes met, the Secret Service agents rushed over and blocked her from view.

Juni had never felt more alone.

CHAPTER 5

The next morning, Juni found himself standing in the hallway at the OSS headquarters, waiting for the president, Gary, Gregorio, and a few Secret Service agents to finish talking to Donnagon about the night before. Juni stared at a framed photograph of himself on the wall. SPY KID OF THE YEAR, it read. As he watched, a janitor removed his picture and replaced it with a photo of Gary.

The door to the interview room opened. "I had the Transmooker device in my hand. But . . . Juni wanted to claim it for himself," Juni heard Gary say as the agents stepped out.

"Okay," said Donnagon. "That should do it. Thanks, son."

The president wrung his hands. "If that doomsday device falls into the wrong hands, we're all *doomed*!" he exclaimed.

"Thank you, Mr. President. That will be all," Donnagon said. The Secret Service agents took the president by the elbows and escorted him down the hall.

"Doomed!" the president called back over his shoulder.

"Understood, sir," said Donnagon. He barely glanced at Juni, then strode off down the hallway, leaving Juni and Gregorio alone.

Juni looked at his father. "Whatever Gary told you is a lie. I was in the right. You'd have done the same."

Gregorio grimly handed him a piece of paper. "You've been temporarily . . . disavowed," he said, then added, "It was not my idea."

Juni scanned the paper. "You mean, I've been *fired*?"

Gregorio nodded. "Signed by Donnagon himself."

"And you couldn't stop it?" Juni looked his father in the eye, hard.

Gregorio flinched under his son's stare. "I don't have . . . that kind of power," he tried to explain. "But I think it will be good for a while. Give us time to sort things out."

Without taking his eyes from his father's, Juni removed his Level Two badge and handed it to

Gregorio. A group of kids passing in the hallway turned and stared at him. They'd never seen a Spy Kid *fired* before!

"Keep an eye on Gary. He's up to no good," Juni warned. Without another word, he turned and walked away.

Later that afternoon, Juni was slumped at the kitchen table. Even a new episode of his favorite TV show, *Floop's Fooglies*, didn't cheer him up. As he despondently stared at the TV, Juni's Thumb Thumb valet waddled over on its two thumb legs, holding a cup of soup for Juni between its two thumb arms. The Cortezes had inherited the strange creature when they helped stop Floop's diabolical plan to take over the world. Juni thanked the Thumb Thumb, but pushed the soup aside. He wasn't feeling very hungry.

Carmen came into the kitchen and watched the show over Juni's shoulder. On the screen, two robots that looked like Carmen and Juni linked arms and smiled. The robots were another of Floop's inventions. He had originally created them to be weapons, but Juni had convinced him that they would be better on his television show.

"We're pretty good, aren't we?" Carmen said to Juni, nodding at the robots.

Juni barely managed to smile. "I was fired," he told her.

"I know," said Carmen. "I hacked into the OSS data files and saw the news." She dunked a piece of bread in Juni's soup and gobbled it down. "It was partly my fault, I suppose," she added. "I'm sorry."

"Well," said Juni. "I guess that's that."

Carmen looked at her brother's miserable expression. "Let's go to the tree house," she said. "I've got an idea."

"I guess I could always set up a small detective agency out here or something," Juni said glumly as Carmen led the way outside to the giant oak tree in the backyard.

"You're thinking small again, Juni," she said. Together they entered a secret door at the base of the oak tree. Inside the trunk was an elevator. A computer scanned Carmen's and Juni's faces to identify them.

"*Your name?*" it asked Carmen.

"Carmen Elizabeth Juanita Echo Sky Brava Cortez," Carmen said, using her full name.

"*Verified*," the computer said. "*Your name?*" it asked Juni.

"Juni Rocket Racer Rebelde Cortez." The elevator doors slid open, and the kids stepped inside.

At the top of the tree house, the elevator doors opened onto a huge control center, filled with every gadget a kid could imagine, and some they might never have dreamed of. Carmen and Juni's uncle Machete, who made the coolest spy gadgets in the world, had built the tree house for them.

As Carmen sat down at a computer workstation, Juni picked up a drawing of a strange creature that he'd been working on before the banquet. "I'm kinda looking forward to re-tirement," he told Carmen. "I can get back to all the projects and dreams I left behind." He picked up a crayon and began to color the drawing.

"Stop it, Juni," Carmen said impatiently. "Do you want your job back or not?" Juni looked at her curiously. Did she mean what he thought she meant? "That's right," Carmen said. "Reinstated. Level Two. So we can get back the missing Transmooker device."

"How?" Juni asked.

Carmen turned and began punching codes into the computer keyboard. Suddenly, the window behind Juni transformed into a giant computer screen.

"Welcome to the OSS agency's top secret files!" said the computer. *"How can we help you?"*

CHAPTER 6

As Juni watched, Carmen hacked into the OSS surveillance system. The hallway at the OSS agency headquarters suddenly appeared on the computer screen. Gary and Gerti Giggles stood in the hallway, shaking hands with different officials.

"Looks like Gary and Gerti are about to get a briefing on the Ukata assignment," said Carmen. She watched as the Giggleses disappeared behind a closed door. "We should listen in. Is RALPH still at your office?"

Juni nodded. "If they haven't cleaned it out yet." He typed a remote-control code into Carmen's keyboard. Miles away in Juni's office at the agency, RALPH blinked to life.

"Transferring data," said Carmen. She pushed a few more keys. Picking up the signal, RALPH scurried over to the door and slid underneath.

In the headquarters hallway, the little robot shot out a web, attaching itself to the leg of a person walking by. A few paces down the hallway, RALPH leaped from the person's leg onto a maintenance cart. From there it scrambled up to the door of the room where Gary and Gerti were being briefed. Shooting out another web, RALPH attached itself to the ceiling.

With RALPH as a spy camera, Carmen and Juni could now see and hear everything in the briefing room. They leaned forward in their chairs as Donnagon described the assignment.

"There is a Bermuda Triangle off the coast of Madagascar," he was saying. He pointed to a computerized map. "As you may remember, this is an area where some of our OSS cargo ships have been disappearing for more than a year." On the map, a graphic image of a cargo ship sailed toward an area of ocean and suddenly disappeared.

"Survivors of these disappearances tell delusional tales of a mysterious island, populated by strange creatures," Donnagon went on. "Obviously, no landmass is located anywhere near that area, so such tales were often dismissed. However, the magnet ship that captured the Transmooker . . ." Donnagon's face grew serious, "was last seen in that same area."

On the map, a graphic of the magnet ship flew over the same body of water and faded out.

"We need a small ship, piloted by two small agents, to get a closer look. If you find anything out of the ordinary, return and report it. Repeat. You find something, you report it here."

Gary and Gerti nodded in agreement. "We accept," they said in unison.

In the tree house, Carmen nodded as well. "You bet we accept." Typing into the computer, she told RALPH to come home, then clicked back to the OSS mainframe. She searched through the database until she came to a list titled, "Duty Assignments." She scrolled down to "Carmen and Juni."

"It's a great assignment," Juni said unhappily. "But Gary and Gerti have it . . . and I'm fired."

"I'm reassigning you to the OSS," Carmen told him, typing away on her keyboard.

Juni's eyes opened wide. "Don't tell me your hacking into—"

"Already done," said Carmen. She turned to him with a triumphant smile. "Level Two status *reinstated*."

Juni leaped to her side, horrified. "Carmen, you can't do this!" he cried. "We'll be banned from the OSS forever!"

Carmen ignored this comment. "We'll assign ourselves the Ukata assignment, and program a new destination for Gary and Gerti."

Juni hesitated. Then he grinned. "Now *that* I've got to be a part of." He rushed over to his computer console and clicked a few buttons. Gary's personal data files came up on the screen.

"*State name, please*," said the computer.

"Gary Giggles," Juni said in Gary's voice. The computer began to bleep. A warning light flashed red.

"It's not working," Carmen told him. "It knows you're not him."

Juni held up a hand to silence her. Then he laughed Gary's weird laugh.

"*Identity confirmed*," said the computer. "*New destination?*"

"How about . . . the Gobi Desert," Juni said.

"Stop it, Juni," Carmen said, frowning.

Juni smirked. "Don't want your boyfriend to go so far away?"

"He's not my boyfriend," she snapped.

"Okay, then," said Juni. He pushed send, and a message flashed across the screen: *Confirmed*. Juni stared at it with a sinking feeling. "What did we just do, again?" he asked.

"The Transmooker device was taken because of us. We're going to get it back so we can clear your name," Carmen told him. "We just have to solve the case before anyone finds out what we're up to. Are you with me?"

Juni hesitated. "Okay," he said at last.

"Then let's go," said Carmen.

They turned to leave, when suddenly the door to the tree house opened. Carmen and Juni quickly switched off their monitors and hit buttons on their belts. Wires shot from their waists up to the ceiling.

A moment later, a tall man with a mustache and a long, dark ponytail entered the room. "Hello?" he called. He looked around the empty room, then glanced up. Carmen and Juni dangled from the ceiling.

"Get down from there," he told them. The kids quickly disengaged their cables and landed beside their uncle Machete.

"Thought you were someone else," Carmen explained.

"Who gave you a key?" asked Juni.

Machete rolled his eyes. "You forgot who built this?" he asked. He held up a box. "I've brought you the very latest in gadgets and spy gear."

"Cool!" said Carmen. "'Cause we're gonna need it." They tore into the box and pulled out a pair of heavy-duty watches.

"The very latest spy watch," Machete told them. "Cell phone, Internet access, satellite TV . . . you name it. It's a total communications center on your wrist. Does everything but tell you what time it is."

Juni looked at him. "It doesn't tell time?"

Machete shrugged. "It's got so much stuffed into it, there was no room left for the clock."

Carmen examined her watch carefully. "Are you sure these are new?" she asked, recalling their experience with Gary and Gerti at the Troublemaker Studios Theme Park. "We can't be running around with outdated equipment."

"An agent's only as good as his gadgets," Juni added.

Machete frowned. "That's not true. You need to be self-sufficient. That's something no gadget in the world can ever replace."

Carmen shrugged. What her uncle said made sense, but there were some really cool gadgets in his box. "That's an interesting concept," she said, holding up another piece of spy gear. "I'll need four of these."

"Close your eyes. Put out your wrist," Machete told Carmen. "I'm gonna give you the one gadget you can never do wrong by." Carmen closed her eyes. Reaching up, Machete pulled out the elastic band holding his ponytail and placed it around Carmen's wrist.

Carmen wrinkled her nose. "A rubber band?"

"Nope. A Machete Elastic Wonder."

"It's a *rubber band*," said Carmen.

"It's also the world's greatest gadget," Machete told her. "Nine hundred ninety-nine uses. And the best thing is that you have to figure out what those uses are. With this." He pointed to Carmen's head.

"He's right," said Juni. "Use number one: a stylish bracelet."

Carmen pulled the rubber band off her wrist. Pressing one end against Juni's arm, she stretched it back. "Use number two," Carmen said. She released the band. *Snap!*

"Ouch," said Juni, rubbing his arm.

Machete smiled. "I'm gonna make a fortune with those," he said.

CHAPTER 7

"Donnagon, I was researching the Ukata assignment," Gregorio said, later that morning at the OSS senior headquarters. He held up a file that he'd been reviewing.

But before he could finish, Donnagon snatched the file away.

"And why were you doing that?" he snapped.

Gregorio looked at him in surprise. "Because that's my job here," he answered. "The files were missing vital information. Sir, it's my recommendation you do not send your children out there. It may be dangerous."

Donnagon eyed Gregorio carefully. "I had originally thought about assigning it to you and Ingrid."

"We don't take active assignments anymore, remember?" Gregorio replied. "That was the deal in our returning to the OSS—no more risks."

"You see? We're all out of heroes," Donnagon

said. "My children can handle it. Besides, they're the only ones small enough to go undetected."

"It will be harder for us to track them if something goes wrong," Gregorio pointed out.

"Nothing is going to go wrong," Donnagon said confidently. "It's all been . . . taken care of." With a little giggle, Donnagon brushed past Gregorio and strode down the hallway. Gregorio watched him go, his eyes narrowed with suspicion.

Meanwhile, Carmen and Juni were sneaking through the loading dock in the OSS vehicle-assignment area. They walked past cars, planes, choppers, submarines, and mini-submarines, keeping an eye out for anyone who might know they shouldn't be there.

"Are you sure this is going to work?" asked Juni.

"Just be cool," Carmen told him. "As far as anyone is concerned, you're back on the force."

At the end of the dock, an engineer was looking over the vehicles. When he turned around, they saw it was Felix Gumm.

"Hi, Uncle Felix!" Carmen said brightly.

"I'm not your uncle," Felix replied.

"I know, it's just easier to call you that," said Carmen. "You don't mind, do you?" Before Carmen and Juni found out that their parents were spies, Felix had kept an eye on them whenever Ingrid and Gregorio had work to do. Carmen and Juni had always thought he was their uncle. Only when their parents' real identities had been revealed, did they discover that Felix actually worked for the OSS, too.

Felix turned to Juni. "Welcome back," he said. He checked the assignment report he was holding. "It says here you were reinstated."

Juni and Carmen glanced at each other nervously. "Yes," Carmen said quickly. "He was fired, then rehired. All in the same day." She presented the OSS checkout tag for their vehicle. Felix looked it over.

"Let me get the keys to *DragonSpy* sub number five," Felix said. He hurried off.

Just then, Carmen and Juni heard a creepy laugh. They turned and saw Gary and Gerti heading for them, carrying their own checkout tag.

"Wow, looking good with that new gear, Carmen," Gary said, looking over the new equipment Uncle Machete had given them.

"Thanks," Carmen said proudly. "It's the latest stuff."

"Very cool," Gerti said. "Only, we had that weeks ago. Here's what's *really* new." Gary and Gerti pulled back their sleeves. Wrapped around their arms were extreme new spy watches. The watches had so many different features installed that they stretched from the kids' wrists all the way up to their elbows.

"Nanotechnology," Gary explained. "Everything you're wearing is right here on my wrist. Super accurate and oh so light. It even . . . tells time."

Juni looked enviously at the brightly lit screens and flashing buttons on the Giggleses' mega-watches. "How did *you* get *that*?" he cried.

"It's a prototype. You can't be running around with those mass-produced gadgets. I always go with prototypes. Sure, they're a little *buggy*. But I can deal." Gary pulled a plastic bag from his pocket and waved the bag in front of Juni. Juni gasped. Inside was the smashed head of his little robot, RALPH.

"I accidentally squashed him on my way out of the OSS building," Gary said, tossing the bag at Juni. "He was outdated, anyway," Gary added. "Consider it a mercy killing."

Just then, Felix returned with their vehicles. "Gary and Gerti Giggles, here is assignment SEIKJu9," he said.

Gary and Gerti climbed into their ship. "Don't hurt yourselves with that outdated gear," Gary called back to Carmen and Juni. "Remember, an agent is only as good as his gadgets." The Giggleses waved at Carmen and Juni as their ship took off.

"Well, do you have this?" Juni shouted furiously. He grabbed the rubber band around Carmen's wrist and held it up.

"Shhh!" Carmen said, snatching her wrist away.

At that moment, Felix brought a minisubmarine over to them. "You've got the Ukata assignment," he said, impressed. "Good luck."

She and Juni climbed into their ship. Seconds later, the engines roared to life. "Thanks, Uncle Felix," said Carmen.

"I'm not your uncle," Felix said as their ship sped away.

CHAPTER 8

"*Welcome to the DragonSpy,*" said a computerized voice as their submarine zoomed through the underground exit tunnels. Carmen and Juni sat at separate control stations, checking out the ship.

"Nice sub," Carmen commented. "Seems like they get more and more sophisticated each month. Everything is automated."

"*Now picking your nose,*" she heard the computerized voice say.

She spun around to face Juni. His back was to her, and a metal claw was moving around near his face. "Juni, what are you doing?" she demanded.

"Nothing," Juni replied. He quickly pushed a button, and the metal claw retracted into the control panel.

Carmen shook her head. "Little brothers," she muttered to herself.

The ship burst to the surface of the ocean and began to skim across the water. Juni watched as the

OSS headquarters receded behind them.

"Let's check our lunch boxes for mission updates," said Carmen. She pushed a button and two metal lunch boxes rose from the sub's center console. When Carmen and Juni swiped their identification badges across the lunch boxes' scanners, the boxes opened. Drink holders popped up and automatically filled their cups, hamburgers unwrapped themselves, and French fries sprouted up from the box, as hot and crispy as if they were fresh from the fryer.

As the lunches made themselves, Juni sat back in his chair, trying to put RALPH back together. "Sorry, RALPH," he told the broken little bug. "You were the best spy on the force."

"Juni, leave it alone. He's a goner," said Carmen.

Juni glared at her. "Thanks to your buddy, Gary."

"It was an accident."

"You like him, *and* believe him?" Juni cried.

"I don't like him," Carmen said, turning back to her computer. When she hit a button, photos of Gary appeared on her computer screen. "That much," she added.

Juni shook his head a few times in disbelief. "How is it we're related?" he asked.

"Juni, you're my brother and I love you," Carmen told him. "But *back* off."

"Gary's a bad guy," Juni warned.

"Maybe I know that," said Carmen. Juni looked at her, confused. "I think I can change him," she explained.

Juni shook his head again. "I don't understand you."

"And you never will," said Carmen.

Just then, a neon-green lollipop rose up from a holder in each of their lunch boxes. "Lollipop synchronization," said Carmen. Simultaneously, they bit into their lollipops. Inside they each found a tiny slip of paper.

"'TMD location determined by Island Man,'" Carmen read.

"Mine says, 'Beware slizzards and sporks,'" said Juni. He looked at Carmen. The message sounded like nonsense.

"These were meant for Gerti and Gary," Carmen reminded him. "It must have been part of the briefing we missed. I'll figure it out." She turned to her computer, and began hacking into the OSS files. As she read through a document, her brow wrinkled.

"Strange," she said, "Tales of a mysterious island. Disappearing ships, mysterious creatures . . . and yet no info anywhere on the OSS cargo, or the missing magnet ship." She clicked through more information. Suddenly, a photo appeared on her screen. "Check this out," she said, transferring the image to Juni's computer.

The photo showed Donnagon and a mysterious man. Their heads were bent together, studying the Transmooker device. "I don't get it," said Juni. "What's Donnagon doing there? He wasn't OSS director yet." He glanced at Carmen. "Still think your boyfriend is a hero?"

Carmen ignored him. "There's only one person I know of who can help us with old OSS secrets," she said.

"Who?" asked Juni. Carmen smiled.

On the set of *Floop's Fooglies*, Floop was dancing atop a candy-colored cube. A cluster of Thumb Thumbs twirled around him and a chorus of other weird creatures sang in the background. Suddenly, the strange performance was interrupted by a ringing cell phone.

Floop pulled his phone from his pocket. "Yes?" he shouted above the din.

"Hello, Floop. Juni Cortez speaking," came the voice at the other end of the line.

"One moment, please," said Floop. He put the phone down and shouted, *"Cut!"* The singing and dancing stopped. "That's better," said Floop, raising the phone to his ear. "What can I do for you?" he asked Juni. "I mean, you've done so much for me. Your robot counterparts are the surprise hit characters of the entire show."

"Actually, Carmen wants a word with Minion," Juni said.

"He's right here, practicing a four-part harmony," Floop said.

Minion took the phone in an eight-fingered hand and held it to one of the ears on his four heads. Once, Minion had been a normal-looking man with a sinister plot to take over the OSS . . . and the world! With Floop's help, Juni and Carmen had stopped him, but unfortunately Minion had ended up with a few extra heads in the process. Now he worked as an extra on Floop's TV show.

"*Bueno,*" Minion said into the phone.

"Carmen Cortez speaking. How ya doing, Minion?"

"It's a little Floopy around here for my taste," Minion told her. "But it's a living."

"I need information on your favorite subject. The OSS," Carmen said.

Meanwhile, Juni's mind was on other things. "I need to make a call," he told Carmen.

She nodded and waved him off.

Using his computer, Juni dialed Alexandra's number on the ship's communication system.

"*To send a message to the president's daughter, press one. . . .*" the computer said. Juni had reached the answering service. He pressed "one." The system started recording.

"Hello, Alexandra. It's me, Agent Juni Cortez. I'm out on a mission. I know I shouldn't be ... but I'm trying to do something heroic again. But it might end up being something really dumb. So if it's dumb, forgive me."

Juni paused. Little did he know that Alexandra was in her room in the White House, screening her calls. She lay on her bed, watching Juni on a large screen as he continued his message.

"I ... uh ... had an idea for you getting to talk with your dad." Alexandra sat up and leaned closer to the screen. "Simply tell him you need to talk to him. Tell him it's nothing urgent, but someday it might be, and you need to open the communication lines now. I think he'll understand."

Alexandra reached out to pick up the connector, so she could talk to Juni. But just then, the image wobbled and became fuzzy.

On board the *DragonSpy*, Juni and Carmen felt a crash that shook the whole ship.

"Something's wrong, Juni. Take the wheel!" cried Carmen.

"Gotta go! Good luck!" Juni shouted to Alexandra a moment before his computer shut down. He took over the steering as Carmen continued her call with Minion.

"So what do you make of this?" she asked.

"Smells like the work of Donnagon Giggles," Minion told her. "He had first contact with the Transmooker technology."

"You think Donnagon is behind this?" Carmen asked in surprise.

"Hey, kid. You're talking to a man with four heads," said Minion. "Trust me, the guy's dirt."

"So what should we look for?" Carmen asked.

"Find the island. Then, find the Island *Man*. That would have been Donnagon's first contact."

"Will do. Thanks, Minion," Carmen said.

"Be a good girl and swat your brother," Minion added.

"Oh, I will," Carmen promised. She hung up. "We're nearing destination zone," she told Juni. "The location radius where the disappearance occurred is right . . . here."

Just as she pointed to the digital map, the lights blinked out beneath her finger. A second later, the entire submarine shut down! Red emergency lights flared and went out. The sub began to rock back and forth in the deep water. Looking out the window, Carmen and Juni could see their sub was sinking. Fast.

"Hold on to something!" Carmen shouted.

With a jarring thud, the ship hit the ocean floor. Water began to trickle in. Quickly, Juni snatched up his sticky lollipop and used it to patch the hole.

Meanwhile, Carmen was frantically hitting buttons on the control panel. But it was no use. "All power is off, even the emergency, " she told Juni. "My flashlight won't even work."

In the darkness, they could hear water pouring into their cabin from other leaks. They cracked glow sticks and placed breather grips over their faces.

"Let's get outta here," Carmen said.

They began to work their way toward the rear of the rapidly flooding ship. When they reached the gear room, they sealed off the entrance to keep out the water.

Juni examined the equipment by the eerie green light of the glow stick. A row of survival packs in different sizes lined the rack. "How do you want to travel?" he asked. "Light or heavy?"

"Let's go heavy," Carmen said. "We may not be coming back here." They pulled the largest packs off the rack, then climbed into baggy inflatable suits and placed air domes over their faces. Juni checked the breathing valve and gulped in a puff of air.

"At least the mask works," he reported.

"I think its because they're valve operated," Carmen replied. "Not electrical or mechanically based."

The ship was rapidly filling with water. It was time to go. Carmen pressed a button to launch them from the ship, but nothing happened. She reached overhead and used her hands to pry open the hatch. Water poured in.

"Good luck," Juni said.

"You, too. Stay close," Carmen told him. She pulled her mask over her head just as the room flooded. Together, Carmen and Juni paddled out the hatch into the ocean.

As soon as they'd left the ship, Carmen and Juni's inflatable suits began to fill with air. They zoomed upward through the water until they exploded out of the ocean like two giant balloons.

Juni and Carmen bobbed on the surface. Their hands and faces looked like tiny dots on the enormous beach balls of their inflated suits. With difficulty, Juni reached his swollen arm up to his face and tore off his mask. "Was that supposed to happen?" he asked Carmen.

"The suits have an electrical shutoff, which didn't work," she replied. "Good thing we ran our of air or they would have exploded."

The two kids looked around them. In every direction, sparkling blue water stretched away as far as the eye could see. There was no land in sight.

Nonetheless, Juni smiled. "Well, we can still laugh," he told his sister.

"At what?" asked Carmen.

"At whatever you imagine Gary and Gerti are doing right now."

At that moment, Gary and Gerti Giggles were standing in the hot sun of the Gobi Desert, realizing that someone had stolen their assignment—and they knew exactly who had done it!

As they stood there, a camel spit at Gerti. She jerked back, knocking into Gary. Together they tumbled into a big, stinky pile of camel poop.

"Someone's gonna pay!" Gerti shouted, shaking her smelly fist. "Someone's gonna pay!"

A little avalanche of dung tumbled down the

heap and plopped on Gary's head. He bared his teeth and growled. "Cortezes!"

CHAPTER 10

Back at OSS headquarters, Ingrid and Gregorio were moving files into Gregorio's new office.

"I like your new office," Ingrid said, looking around at the closet-sized work space Donnagon had assigned him. "It's . . . smaller, but cozier." She smiled encouragingly.

"Mr. Cortez," a voice came from the intercom on the desk. "Your children left a message for you earlier. They said that they'll be a little late for dinner tonight."

"Thank you," Gregorio said.

"So many successful missions," Ingrid stated as she sorted through a pile of paperwork from past missions.

"Amazing, isn't it?" Gregorio agreed. He held up a photo. "Remember this one? The two spies who saved the world?"

Ingrid smiled. "There was only one thing we never truly accomplished."

"What's that?" Gregorio asked.

"We never got my parents' full blessing." Ingrid glanced cautiously at Gregorio. Her parents were a sore subject with him.

Gregorio frowned. "Saving the world is one thing. Impressing your parents . . . now that's *impossible*," he replied. Ingrid's parents had never liked him. And to tell the truth, Gregorio wasn't all that fond of them, either.

"I'd like to invite them down," Ingrid said. "They want to see their grandchildren, and I think you deserve another chance to show them that—"

Gregorio held up a hand. "Invite them if you want, but I won't be here. Tell them I had to go on another mission . . . to the *moon*." Suddenly, a horrible thought crossed his mind. "You invited them already, didn't you?"

"No, I—" Before Ingrid could finish her reply, Donnagon's face appeared on Gregorio's computer and telecommunications screens.

"Cortezes," he said. "I have some pretty bad news. May I come in?"

"Of course," said Gregorio.

A moment later, Donnagon appeared in the doorway of Gregorio's office. "Two of our Spy Kids operatives are lost. The Ukata assignment."

Gregorio looked concerned "Your children had that assignment."

"We're so sorry, Donnagon," said Ingrid. "How can we help?"

"Actually, my children are safe. Somewhere in the Gobi Desert, I believe," Donnagon told them. Ingrid and Gregorio glanced nervously at each other. If Gary and Gerti weren't on the Ukata assignment, then who was?

"I'm sorry to say that Carmen and Juni are somehow the ones on the Ukata assignment. A computer error of some sort," said Donnagon.

The Cortezes stared at him, mouths hanging open. Ever since their kids had started training as spies, they had worried that one day something would go wrong on a mission. Now their worst fears had come true.

"Communications?" Ingrid finally managed to ask.

"None. Their *DragonSpy* ship doesn't show up on radar or satellite." He looked at them sorrowfully. "You two risked your lives to save me once before. Let me now go and get your children back."

Gregorio shook his head. This was a job he didn't dare trust to anyone else. "Thank you, Donnagon, but respectfully, we'll have to go ourselves," he said. "If you could arrange tactical backup and surveillance support of our efforts, we'll leave immediately."

As Ingrid and Gregorio headed for the door, Donnagon called after them. "Oh, and Ingrid? I know this may be a bad time, but your parents are here."

Moments later, Ingrid and Gregorio were in the OSS vehicle-assignment dock, loading a spy sub with every spy gadget known to man. Ingrid's parents, Helga and Valentin, followed them around.

"But we *want* to help!" Helga told her daughter. "They're our only grandchildren." She pressed her lips tightly together as Ingrid's father whispered something in her ear. "Oh, *they* don't count," she snapped at him.

Gregorio silently went about his work, trying to ignore them. "We'll be back as soon as possible," Ingrid said. "This is a dangerous assignment, Mother, so wait here."

"You need us," said Helga.

Valentin moved his wheelchair closer to the spy sub. "We taught you everything you know, Ingrid," he said. "But not everything *we* know."

Ingrid blew them a kiss. "See you in a few hours." She hit the door to the sub. Gregorio waved good-bye to Ingrid's parents as it closed.

As the sub blasted off, Helga shook her head. "I still don't like him," she said.

CHAPTER
11

At that moment, Carmen and Juni were still bobbing like buoys far out in the Indian Ocean. Unable to swim with her puffed-up arms, Carmen paddled with her feet. Juni jogged through the water behind her, trying to keep up.

Suddenly, Carmen looked up, bewildered. "Juni? Was that there before?" she asked.

Juni followed her eyes. No more than a few hundred meters away an island rose up from the water! Dense green trees surrounded a large volcano at its center.

Suddenly Juni felt something move against his foot. "Are you kicking me?" he asked Carmen.

"I'm way over here!" Carmen called back.

Juni saw a blur of movement in the water beneath him. "There's something under me!" he exclaimed. "Come look! Do you see it?"

Awkwardly, Carmen paddled over to him and looked down. "No," she replied.

As Juni and Carmen peered into the blue-green water, a huge sea monster rose up behind them. Its dripping scales glinted in the sunlight as it looked hungrily at the two kids.

But Carmen and Juni didn't notice. They were too busy trying to figure out how to get to shore. "Let's see. It's about two hundred yards. If we kick steadily at a foot per kick, we'll reach it in. . . ." Carmen paused, trying to do the math. Behind them, the monster opened its mouth. It was going to swallow the Cortez kids whole!

As the monster hovered over them, Juni counted on his fingers. "Twenty-five minutes?" he guessed.

"I don't know," said Carmen. "My calculator doesn't work."

Snap! The monster's jaws clamped shut, its razor fangs missing the kids' bodies by inches. *Whoosh!* Air gushed from their punctured suits, sending Carmen and Juni shooting through the water toward the island.

Wham! They slammed onto the shore. For a moment, they lay in the sand, catching their breath. Then they peeled off their deflated suits and began to haul their packs up the beach.

Juni glared at Carmen as he tugged the heavy,

wet pack across the sand. "'Let's travel heavy,'" he said, mimicking his sister. "Good idea."

"Give it a rest," she snapped back. "Let's make a fire and build a shelter." Reaching into her pack, she pulled out a small silver disk. She tossed it onto a pile of sticks. Nothing happened. Carmen pulled out a remote control and clicked it at the disk, but the instant fire starter refused to start. She tossed a bag onto the sand, hoping that it would spring into an instant shelter. But, again, nothing.

Carmen shivered in her wet clothing. "This is unbelievable," she cried. She checked her watch. It, too, was dead.

"Maybe it's the island," Juni suggested.

"Some sort of cloaking device, you think?" Carmen looked around thoughtfully. "A force strong enough to remove it from radar and disable our equipment so"—her eyes widened—"none of our gadgets work."

Juni stared at her in horror. "No gadgets? You mean, we're gonna have to use our heads?"

"Yes," Carmen replied. She tossed Juni two sticks.

"Ouch," said Juni.

As Carmen and Juni set to work building a fire, a pair of eyes peered out at them from the bushes.

Little did the kids know that they weren't alone on the sandy beach. A man from the magnet ship was watching.

Back at the OSS headquarters, Donnagon was admiring his huge new office when a call came in on his communications screen. He leaped to his desk and faced the image. It was one of the men from the magnet ship!

"Did you find the source of equal or greater power?" Donnagon asked him.

"We did," the Magna Man replied. "It emanates from the north side of the island. We'll need extractors."

Donnagon nodded. "Have you located the Island Man?" he asked.

"Not yet," the Magna Man replied. "He's somewhere underground."

"Start digging. I'm on my way." Donnagon clicked off the screen. He leaned comfortably back in his chair, buffing his nails and examining a digital map of the island. Thoughtfully, he picked up a pen and circled the north side. Donnagon smiled to himself.

A short time later, Gary and Gerti's submarine returned from the Gobi Desert. Donnagon and Felix held their noses as the smelly, dung-covered kids climbed out of the sub.

"Are you kids all right?" Donnagon asked. "You were somehow accidentally sent to the wrong place."

"There was no *accident*, Dad," Gary said irritably. "The Cortez kids switched assignments on us."

"That's not possible, is it?" Donnagon asked. Felix shook his head.

"Wake up, Dad," Gerti snapped. "Carmen's a *hacker*! Of course they did it."

Donnagon frowned. "Well, Juni and Carmen are now missing in action. So you should feel lucky."

"Really?" Gary and Gerti looked at each other. Then, without so much as a "see you later," they turned around and climbed back into the submarine.

"Where are you going?" Donnagon asked.

"Where do you think?" said Gary. "After them."

CHAPTER 12

Gary and Gerti's ship hurtled through the ocean water. Fish bounced off its windshield, like bugs off a speeding car. Gerti watched over Gary's shoulder as he gunned the motor.

"How fast are you going?" she asked.

Gary looked at the speedometer. "Eighty-five knots," he told her. The sub smashed through a coral reef. They were going so fast that the whole ship had started to shake.

"Well, go faster," Gerti told him.

Gary smiled. "My pleasure." He gripped the speed lever and pushed it all the way forward.

"Faster, faster, faster!" Gerti shouted.

"*Nearing destination*," a computerized voice told them.

Slam! Their ship came to a dead halt. Gary and Gerti flew forward and smacked the windshield. The lights went out. The engines died. The submarine quietly sank to the bottom of the ocean.

Carmen and Juni Cortez are top agents of the OSS.
Don't mess with these Spy Kids!

Trouble begins at Troublemaker Studios Theme Park. The
president's daughter has stolen the top-secret Transmooker
device. Carmen and Juni are called in to help.

Carmen and Juni learn about the Ukata assignment.

In the *DragonSpy* sub, the seasoned
Spy Kids take off on their mission.

Gary and Gerti Giggles are top spy competition.
They follow the Cortezes to Leeke Leeke Island.

Mom and Dad find out that their kids are in serious
danger. Grandma and Grandpa want to help, too.
Now it's a family operation!

Romero hides out on the island. He shows the Spy Kids his
creepy misfit creatures—no wonder he hides out in a cave!

The Giggleses are close behind Carmen and Juni. Gary has
had a "dung" bad day, and his inflate-a-suit has overexpanded.
He has to get to Leeke Leeke Island fast!

Gerti and Gary arrive on Romero's island, ready for revenge.

Carmen and Juni use Romero's map of the island to find the stolen Transmooker. Since their spy gadgets don't work on the island, they'll have to use their heads!

Battling pirate skeletons?! Juni is tempted to take their priceless medallion.

Look out! Romero's creatures are everywhere.

Saving the world is all in a day's work!

Gerti looked at Gary. "Now what?"

Minutes later, Gary and Gerti burst out of the ocean, wearing huge, puffy inflate-a-suits. Their tiny heads and hands looked ridiculous on the giant beach balls of their bodies. But the Giggleses weren't giggling. They were furious. The salty seawater made the dung on their clothes and hair smellier than ever.

As they bobbed angrily in the water, the giant sea monster rose up behind them. It opened its enormous mouth. Saliva dripped from its swordlike fangs. Sensing that something was behind them, Gary and Gerti slowly turned around.

"Aaaaaaaaaaah!" they screamed. Their puffy arms flapped frantically. The monster was only inches away.

But just then, the sea monster caught a whiff of the dung-covered kids. It stopped and sniffed at them. Its giant tongue flopped out in disgust. With a roar, it sank below the water.

The movement of its body created a monster-sized wave that washed Gary and Gerti to shore. *Wham!* Their inflate-a-suits exploded as their bodies crashed against the sand. Gary struggled to his feet and whipped out his NanoTech SPYwatch. "I'm gonna blast that sucker to *bits*," he growled. As the sea monster leaped into the air, he aimed the watch's laser function at the creature and pressed the trigger.

But nothing happened. Gary hit the laser switch again. The watch fell apart in his hands. Furious, Gary threw the watch to the ground and began to march out into the water, ready to fight the monster one-on-one. But Gerti held him back.

"Save it for the Cortezes," she told him.

"Good idea," Gary said. He spun around. Carmen and Juni's campsite stood in the sand a few feet away. He could see their footprints leading off into the jungle. Gary smiled. "Excellent idea."

Meanwhile, Carmen and Juni were exploring the island. As they crept through the dense undergrowth, they stopped now and then to listen to the strange, creepy sounds that echoed through the jungle. They sounded sort of like animals, though no animals Carmen or Juni had ever heard before.

Suddenly, just as they neared a volcano, Juni heard a different sound.

"Listen. I heard something. Like humming . . ."

Carmen listened, but heard nothing. "A bird?" she asked.

"No," said Juni. "It's mechanical." He heard it again: a distant *put-put-put* like a helicopter.

"Impossible," Carmen said. "We've already determined that nothing mechanical or electric can—" Before she could finish her sentence, Juni grabbed her and pulled her to the ground. A second later, a strange hovercraft flew overhead. Peering up through a cover of leaves, Juni caught his breath. At the controls was one of the men from the magnet ship!

They watched as the hovercraft disappeared through a doorway in the side of the volcano. Then Carmen turned to Juni. "Someone has power here," she said. "We need to find out *who* and for *what*."

Hurrying through the forest, they soon reached the volcano. They looked around for the place where the hovercraft had disappeared. But all they saw was smooth rock. There was no entrance at all.

"I don't get it," said Carmen. "I saw it go through this wall. What's your assessment, Juni?"

"I think we've been set up," Juni replied. "If Donnagon is behind this . . . he knew all along you'd hack your way into taking that assignment."

Carmen nodded. "I was wondering the same thing. What else?"

Juni frowned. "I think better with food in my belly," he told Carmen. "If RALPH was here, he could figure this out," he added as he pulled a snack-meal bar from his pocket. Suddenly, a strange, loud roar echoed through the jungle. Carmen and Juni looked up. Some sort of creature was coming through the trees, moving fast!

"Higher ground, Juni!" Carmen yelled. Juni pocketed the snack, and the two kids hurried up the side of the volcano.

From the top, they could see out over the entire island. Strange winged creatures skimmed through the air above the trees. All around, the dense foliage shifted and swayed, as if large beasts were moving through the jungle below.

Juni climbed over to the edge of the volcano and peered down inside.

Carmen followed him. "Get away from there," she said anxiously.

"It doesn't appear to be active," Juni said. Just

then, a rumble shook the volcano. Juni lost his balance and tumbled inside!

Quick as lightning, Carmen attached a line to the edge and dove after him. She managed to grab hold of one of his untied shoelaces. The two kids dangled helplessly in the air above the pit. The volcano rumbled again, shaking Carmen's safety line.

"What are you waiting for?" Juni asked.

"If my auto retractor was functioning, I could get us both back up," Carmen told him. Juni struggled up and began to climb over his sister. But just as he grasped the line, he noticed something frightening. The line was starting to unravel!

"Why did you stop? Anything wrong?" asked Carmen.

With a sinking feeling, Juni watched as the last threads came apart. "Close your eyes," he warned his sister.

"Why?" she asked. *Snap!* The line gave way.

"Juni!" Carmen cried, grasping through the air for his hand.

"What?"

"I'm sorry!"

Juni and Carmen plummeted down into the dark volcano.

Several hours later, Carmen and Juni were still tumbling through the air. "How long have we been falling?" Carmen finally asked.

Juni glanced at his watch, then remembered that it didn't tell time. "Three hours?" he guessed.

"Feels like four," said Carmen.

Juni nodded and rubbed his stomach. He was starting to feel hungry. Suddenly he remembered the freeze-dried snack he'd stuck in his pocket hours before. He pulled it out and began to unwrap it.

Carmen looked at him in amazement. "How can you eat?"

He shrugged. "You know that tickling sensation you get when you fall?"

"Of course," said Carmen.

"That pretty much went away after the first hour." He lifted the bar to his lips.

Just then, Carmen cried, "Ground!"

Juni looked down and saw the ground rushing

toward them. He dropped the snack and covered his eyes.

Whomp! They stopped. Realizing he was still in one piece, Juni slowly removed his hands from his face. They were floating in midair!

Carmen looked around in astonishment. Below them a miniature volcano blasted smoky air. The powerful gust was holding them aloft!

As the smoke from the volcano cleared, they saw they were inside a cave. The walls around them were covered in ancient Aztec carvings. Suddenly, Carmen realized they were being watched! A mysterious figure peeked out at them from behind a pillar of lava rock. "Who are you?" she called out.

"What do you want?" a voice said.

"I want to get down," Carmen replied. There was a pause, then a man cautiously crept out from behind the rock. He seemed to be dressed in primitive clothing. But as Carmen and Juni looked more closely, they realized he was wearing a ragged suit and a dirty, tattered lab coat.

Carmen spoke up first. "I'm Carmen Cortez, Special Agent in the OSS."

"I'm . . . Romero. Sole inhabitant of this Leeke Leeke Island," the man replied. He spoke slowly and awkwardly, as if he hadn't talked to anyone in a very long time. He looked at Juni. "And you are?"

"Tired and hungry," Juni answered.

"Nice to meet you," Romero said. He reached out toward a pillar of lava rock and flipped a switch, cutting off the gust of air that kept Carmen and Juni hovering above the miniature volcano. They tumbled out of the air and rolled down the volcano.

"Be careful! You'll crush my island!" Romero cried. The two kids flipped acrobatically and landed on their feet as gracefully as cats.

"Sorry," Carmen said, tiptoeing carefully around the model island that surrounded the volcano. "But we just fell for four hours. We're a little clumsy." She took a step toward Romero. He flinched and backed away.

"You weren't falling," he told her. "It was an illusion."

An illusion? Carmen and Juni looked up in surprise. Sure enough, the opening to the real volcano was only a few hundred meters above them.

"Magic?" asked Juni in awe.

Romero shook his head and hit the switch again. Another burst of air exploded from the top of the miniature volcano. "Science. I made it to scare off unwanted visitors." As Juni moved closer to examine the switch, Romero edged away from him. He was afraid of them!

Just then, a creepy, inhuman cry echoed through the chamber. Romero gasped. "Quickly. We must go someplace safe," he cried. He led the way up a flight of stairs and disappeared through a door in an elaborate Aztec carving. Carmen and Juni followed closely on his heels.

The path opened out into a rough shack furnished with laboratory equipment. As the kids watched, Romero pulled an object from a corner and placed it on a table in front of them. It was a small cage made of clay, dirt, twigs, and metal.

"I'm a genetic specialist. I need a controlled environment for my genetic experiments," Romero explained.

Carmen raised her eyebrows as his meaning dawned on her. "The creatures we've been hearing?"

Romero nodded. "My experiments. Run amok."

"What happened?" asked Juni.

Romero opened the door to the cage. Carmen and Juni gasped as a row of miniature animals walked out onto the table. A mouse-sized lion opened its mouth and roared as a tiny monkey scampered past. They were real live creatures, and yet they were so small they could fit in the palm of a child's hand!

"I thought I'd make a fortune from it," Romero told them. "Kids everywhere would have their own miniature zoos, right there in their bedrooms. Romero's Zoo, I called it."

Juni watched, wide-eyed, as a tiny elephant stood on its hind legs and trumpeted. "Unbelievable," he said. He picked up a little wooden barrel. Three little chimpanzees with their arms linked together tumbled out.

"Monkeys in a barrel," Juni said admiringly.

"Careful!" Romero warned as the chimps leaped onto Juni's head and scurried into his hair. Carmen poked through his hair and plucked them out.

"One day, I accidentally mixed up two or three different test tubes and created a new species," Romero went on. He led them over to another cage. "I became fascinated with the possibilities. I decided I would create a second zoo . . . 'Romero's Zoo Too.'" He opened the door to the cage. Out walked a number of tiny creatures, the likes of which Carmen and Juni had never seen.

A horselike insect buzzed around Juni's head. "Horse-fly?" he guessed. Romero nodded. "Catfish? Spider-monkey?" Juni said, pointing to more creature combinations. A creature with the head of a snake and a muscular, iguanalike body crawled up. Juni stretched out a hand to pet it.

"Slizzard," Romero told him. "Stay away from those." The creature snapped at Juni's finger, and Juni quickly withdrew his hand.

"I began to think that if only I could make them all a wee bit bigger . . . and that's where things went very wrong." One day, Romero explained, he'd accidentally spilled growth serum all over the Zoo Too creatures. In seconds they grew into giant beasts, tearing the roof off his laboratory and escaping. Now they roamed the island freely.

"I've been locked up in here ever since," the scientist told them. "I'm afraid to go out there again. They've tried to gobble me up on more than one occasion. Why do they despise me so?" He looked sadly at his strange creations. "Do you think God stays in heaven because He, too, lives in fear of what He has created here on earth?"

Carmen and Juni glanced at each other. The scientist seemed more than a little wacky to them. Romero frowned when he saw the looks on their faces.

"I'm no loon," he told them.

Loon or not, he still had some more explaining to do. Carmen decided it was time to get to the bottom of things. "What I'm trying to figure out is why this island doesn't show up on even our most advanced satellites," she said.

"I created a cloaking device that would shield my island from curious eyes," Romero replied. "Anything electronically powered that comes within a mile radius instantly shuts down. And any radar that passes over me is displaced, creating the illusion that my island doesn't exist."

Juni snapped his fingers. "The Transmooker device!" he exclaimed.

Romero looked at him in surprise. "How did you know?"

"Your cloaking device is highly coveted," Juni answered. "People everywhere are trying to get their hands on it."

But before Juni could explain further, a scream split the air. It was quickly followed by another.

"Help!" two voices cried. "Help! Help!"

Carmen turned to Romero. "Are you sure we're the only humans?" she asked.

CHAPTER 14

Romero rushed back to the main cave, carrying the Zoo Too cage under his arm. When he reached the miniature volcano, he stopped and pointed. There at its base, two little figures screamed and waved their arms. They looked like tiny people.

"Two children, judging by their size," Romero said.

"What is this?" Carmen asked.

"A miniature of the island," Romero answered. He opened the Zoo Too cage and shook out the creatures onto the model island. "The center point of the volcano provides a gravitational basis for my miniature creatures to line up exactly to where their larger cloned counterparts are."

"You mean, wherever your miniature creatures are on this model, that's where the bigger ones are outside?" asked Carmen.

"Correct," said Romero. "See? The two intruder children are being chased by a slizzard." Carmen and Juni watched as a four-inch slizzard chased the two tiny figures through the jungle.

"It's Gary and Gerti," said Carmen. The two figures fell into a ditch and disappeared from view. The slizzard stood at the edge, snapping at them.

"Leave 'em," Juni said angrily.

"We have to help them!" Carmen cried.

"They shouldn't be snooping around my island, to begin with," Romero said.

"I'm with you, dude," Juni agreed.

Carmen scowled at them in disbelief. "We have to help them!" she repeated.

"I'm not going out there," Romero's voice squeaked with panic. "I'll be eaten!" He turned and ran back.

Carmen watched him go and shook her head. "What a bizarre man," she said to Juni.

Carmen and Juni found their way back to the volcano's opening. They hurried down the side of the mountain, keeping an eye out for familiar landmarks. At last they found the ditch where Gary and Gerti had fallen. The Giggleses were clinging to a ledge high above the chasm.

"What are you guys doing here?" Juni said casually.

"That's real funny, clown," Gary said. "Get us out." Juni knelt and stretched a hand toward them, but they were out of his reach.

"We tried to activate our micrograpplers, but they didn't deploy," Gerti said.

"Gadgets don't work here," Juni told her.

"We *know* that now. Thanks for the update, idiot," Gary snapped. Juni stood up, glared at him, and walked away.

"Juni, come back here. We have to help them!" Carmen scolded. But Juni had only gone to find a long vine. He tied one end around a tree and attached the other end to his waist. Now he could reach them without falling over the edge. "I'll help them," he muttered to himself. "I want to get him up here so I can push him back over myself."

Just then, he heard Gary say, "Just wait till my father gets here."

Juni's head jerked up. "Your father?" he said. Donnagon was coming. His mind started to race.

Back in Romero's shack, the scientist was cowering under a table when he heard a knock at the door. "Who's there?" he called. Suddenly, the door flew inward, knocked off its hinges by a powerful kick.

"Us," said Carmen. She marched into the room, with Juni, Gary, and Gerti behind her. "Why are you still hiding? We're kids, not monsters."

Romero slowly came out of his hiding place. "What's the difference?" He looked nervously at the Giggleses.

"Relax," Carmen told him. "They're OSS agents as well."

"Level One," Gary added, flashing his badge. Juni glared at him.

"They're Agent Donnagon's kids," said Carmen.

Romero crawled out from under the table. "Agent Donnagon?"

Juni eyed him. "You work for the OSS, don't you?"

"I work for a man named Donnagon," Romero admitted.

Gary and Gerti looked back and forth in confusion. "Who is this?" Gary asked.

Juni ignored him. He fixed the scientist with a stare. "Donnagon is not interested in your creatures," he said.

Romero looked surprised. "He's not?"

"The Transmooker device that hides your

island, that's what Donnagon really wants," Juni told him. "Now that he's head of the OSS, he has the power to take it from you."

Suddenly, Gary stepped between them. "What are you babbling about now, Juni?"

"The Transmooker you got from the president's daughter was just a prototype," Juni told him. "The *real* Transmooker device is on this island. It's more powerful and can shut down all technology on the planet. You said your father is on his way. I think he's coming to pick it up."

Everyone was staring at Juni, so no one noticed that Gerti had picked up one of Romero's notebooks and was silently skimming the pages. She glanced around the room, then slipped the book into her pocket. "You're all liars," she declared.

Gary stepped threateningly toward Juni. "You really think you're going to turn us on our own father?"

But Juni held his ground. "Did your dad tell you the mission you went on was just a setup for Carmen and me?" he asked, tilting his chin challengingly. "Why?"

"He has his reasons. That's what being a good

spy is all about," Gary replied. "Trust no one." He tossed a small, black book at Juni.

Juni read the cover. "'*How to Be a Spy.*' Yes, I know. We've read it," he told Gary.

"Read it again," Gary said.

Juni flipped to the marked page and read, "'A good spy makes no binding connections . . . with family or friends.'" He ripped the page from the book and crumpled it up. "I don't believe in that," he said angrily.

"If you want to be a great spy, you better believe it. My father's a great spy. So let's just grow up," Gary told him. "Whatever Dad's done is what it takes to play in the big world." He turned on his heel and stormed out the door. Gerti followed him.

"He's right," said Carmen.

"Ugh!" Juni groaned. "Why can't you side with me just *once*."

"There are no sides," Carmen told him. "You're right, but he's right, too. That's what being a spy means."

"Well, I don't like it," Juni told her.

"Then quit," Carmen said challengingly.

Juni nodded. "I will."

Carmen rolled her eyes. "Yeah, right."

CHAPTER 15

Meanwhile, Ingrid and Gregorio still hadn't found any trace of their children.

"Donnagon was right," Ingrid said. "Their *DragonSpy* sub doesn't show up on radar."

"I'm not interested in finding their sub," Gregorio said. Grabbing his travel bag, he pulled out photos of Carmen and Juni. Each picture had computer circuitry attached to the back. He shoved the photos into the submarine's computer console. "Remember that year I insisted on doing the children's dental work?" he asked.

Ingrid shuddered. "How can I forget?"

"I installed a nonelectrical tracking device in their teeth. But I haven't been able to test it until now." Gregrio pressed a button, and a map of the ocean appeared on the screen. Two dots—one blue, the other pink—glowed in the middle of the map. He looked at Ingrid proudly.

"It works?" Ingrid cried in amazement.

Gregorio nodded. "According to this, they're in the middle of the ocean."

"Above sea level," Ingrid said, scanning the map. "But where they are on the map, there's no landmass. How can that be?"

Suddenly, Ingrid and Gregorio were thrown off balance as their ship lurched to a halt. The lights fluttered.

"Something's got us," Ingrid said.

Gregorio rushed to a porthole and cautiously peered out. He let out a bloodcurdling scream.

Ingrid gasped. "What is it?"

"Your mother," he groaned.

Ingrid looked out the window. Helga and Valentin had overtaken their submarine in a larger ship. Helga waved at Ingrid from a porthole next to them. "We wanted to join you!" she called through the glass.

"Mom, are you nuts?" Ingrid cried in dismay.

"We needed a bigger boat," Helga said, ignoring her question.

A moment later, the door to Ingrid and Gregorio's submarine slid open, and Valentin entered. "And we brought real food," he told them, holding up a metal container. "None of that freeze-dried stuff." He steered his wheelchair down a ramp. Helga struggled to climb through the porthole window.

"You, son-in-law, make yourself useful," she commanded.

Grimacing, Gregorio tried to help her.

"Why are you here?" Ingrid asked.

"We want to help get our grandchildren back," Helga answered.

"We *will* get our grandchildren back," Valentin corrected her.

At last, Helga made it through the window. She turned to Gregorio to thank him. "Wait a minute. You got something on your lip," she said. Reaching up, she pulled his fake mustache off with a loud *rrrrip!* "Got it!" she cried.

"Mom, Dad, I'm a big girl. I can take care of myself. And Greg and I can take care of finding—"

"You don't seem to understand," Valentin interrupted. "This isn't you and Gregorio simply saving the world again. This time we all have much more to lose if you fail—Carmen and Juni."

At last, Gregorio opened his mouth. "You cannot come with us," he said. "It's too dangerous."

Valentin raised his eyebrows. "Oh, you mean we

can't handle ourselves?" he asked. He pushed a button on his wheelchair. Helga pushed a button on her large beaded bracelet. Instantly, their clothes transformed into high-tech suits. The wheelchair turned into a supercharged machine.

Ingrid looked apologetically at Gregorio. He smiled weakly back at her, then said to Helga, "Can I have my mustache back ... please?" It looked like the grandparents were going with them.

Meanwhile, back in Romero's shack, Carmen and Juni were trying to form a plan.

"If Donnagon really is on his way, we have to destroy the Transmooker," Carmen told Romero. "Where is it?"

Romero pointed out the window toward a high peak on the other side of the island. "Not easy to get to," he told them. "The journey alone is more dangerous than the Transmooker itself." He shivered at the idea of going out among all his fierce creatures.

But Juni placed a map on the table. "Show us," he demanded.

Romero looked at him as if he were crazy.

"You're not afraid of the creatures?"

Juni shook his head. "You just gotta show 'em who's boss."

Realizing they were determined to go, Romero gave them directions to his hovercraft, which was hidden in some bushes outside.

"How will it work?" Juni asked as they raced toward the unfamiliar vehicle.

"Supposedly, it's run magnetically," she answered. "We should be able to ride over a determined path." They leaped into the hovercraft and shot off through the jungle.

As soon as they were gone, Gary and Gerti crept out from behind a tree where they had been hiding. They'd heard everything!

"We've got to get to the Transmooker before they do," Gary said. They pulled branches off another hovercraft hidden in the bushes and sped off after Carmen and Juni.

Inside the volcano's cave, Romero anxiously watched them on his model island. He saw Carmen and Juni zigzag through the trees, with Gary and Gerti hot on their trail. He could also see the creatures moving through the island jungle around them.

"Oh, no!" Romero cried, jumping back and forth in frenzy. The kids were headed right for a horde of . . .

Wham! A huge slizzard slammed down on the hood of Carmen and Juni's hovercraft. The ship rocked back and forth dangerously, almost dumping them out. *Wham! Wham! Wham!* Several more slizzards leaped from the trees onto the hovercraft. As she fought to keep the ship under control, Carmen suddenly realized they had another problem. They were headed straight for a rocky cliff!

Drooling and hissing, the slizzards closed in. Carmen and Juni backed away until they were balanced on the edge of the wildly rocking ship. At the last second, they jumped. The ship crashed into the rocks, taking the slizzards with it.

The hovercraft was destroyed. Bruised and dazed, the slizzards slithered away. Carmen and Juni grabbed the map and their scuba gear and ran.

On board Helga and Valentin's sub, Ingrid's parents were sitting on either side of Gregorio, yelling into his ears as he steered the ship.

"Gregorio, the signal requires that you go around it. Use a different approach!" cried Helga.

"He's not going to listen to you, Mother," said Valentin. "He wants to make sure he loses the kids again."

"You're tracking them all wrong," Helga cried. "Ingrid, tell him he's doing it all wrong."

"Mom, Dad, I told you before and I'll tell you again: *no backseat driving*," Ingrid said. "Oh, turn here, honey," she added to Gregorio. He glared at her.

"Are you sure you're reading that map correctly, Gregorio?" asked Valentin. "Maybe you should go lie down a few minutes and let us take the wheel."

At last, Gregorio could stand it no longer. "I'm reading it right," he told them. "The coordinates correspond to Carmen and Juni's current position. These are *my* children." His voice rose to a shout. "And I will *find* my children *MY WAY*."

For a moment everyone stared at him.

"Blah, blah, blah," Helga said at last. "I can never understand a thing he's saying. Never."

Valentin nodded. "Maybe he *should* lie down. . . ."

In a jungle clearing, Carmen and Juni paused to catch their breath. As she panted for air, Carmen frowned. She had just remembered something. She grabbed a pair of tweezers and turned to Juni.

"Open up," she said. Grabbing his jaw, she reached inside with the tweezers and pried a small device from his back tooth.

"Dad had these installed in case we ever got lost," she explained. She handed the tweezers to Juni. "Take mine out. Hurry."

Juni looked at her, confused. "Why?"

"When we get lost, who saves us?" Carmen asked him.

"Mom and Dad," he replied.

"Exactly," said Carmen. "If Mom and Dad also disappear, no one in the OSS can stop Donnagon from using the Transmooker device."

"Donnagon wants us all together so he can destroy the island and all of us with it, erasing all the evidence," Juni said, suddenly understanding. He rolled the tracking device between his fingers thoughtfully. "It's a big sacrifice," he told Carmen. "Your call."

Carmen thought for a moment. Juni was right. They might never see their parents again. But that was one of the many risks a spy had to take. "Family is sacrifice," she decided. She dropped her locator on the ground and crushed it beneath the heel of her shoe.

Juni looked at the tiny device, his last connection to his parents. Holding it close to his mouth, he whispered, "I love you." Then he picked up a rock and smashed the device to bits.

CHAPTER 16

On board the OSS submarine, Gregorio, Ingrid, and Ingrid's parents watched with dismay as first the pink, then the blue lights disappeared from the ocean map. The monitoring screens went dark. They'd lost Carmen and Juni.

"What do we do?" Ingrid asked.

Gregorio's face sagged with grief. "I don't know," he said.

For the first time since she'd climbed aboard, Helga was silent. Valentin's eyes filled with sadness as he regarded the blank screen. But suddenly his face cleared. He sat forward in his chair.

"Now, Gregorio, don't tell me you didn't have a backup plan," he said. Everyone turned to look at him. "Was Juni wearing that charm necklace I sent him for Christmas?" Valentin asked.

"He never takes it off," Ingrid told him.

Valentin smiled and clapped his hands. "Then we've got him!" he cried. Removing his own necklace, he shoved his identification card into the computer console. "I was worried about Juni's *well-being*," he explained, looking pointedly at Gregorio. "So I placed a tracer inside his necklace." He pushed a button and Juni's information appeared on the screen. A dot showing his location glowed on the map.

"There he is," said Valentin. Helga and Valentin slapped high fives.

Ingrid smiled with relief. "Thanks, Dad," she said.

Valentin turned to his son-in-law. "Sure you don't want me to take the wheel?"

Gregorio clenched his jaw, looked straight ahead, and stepped on the gas.

Meanwhile, back in the clearing, Carmen and Juni were studying the map. For the third time that day, Juni pulled the freeze-dried snack bar from his pocket. He had taken just one bite, when he heard the bushes behind them rustle. Juni turned. One of the Zoo Too creatures was standing behind them! It had a face like an ape, but in place of its arms were eight huge spiderlike legs. In one of its front legs, it held a long wooden staff. Juni saw that one of its legs was hurt.

Carmen grabbed Juni's arm and started to pull him away, but Juni stopped her. He looked closely at the creature's dark, gorillalike face. "Hold still," he said. "Maybe it's friendly."

The spider-ape stared at Juni for a moment. Then it opened its mouth and let out a terrifying screech!

"Maybe it's not. Let's go *now*!" Carmen cried. The kids slowly backed away. But for every two steps they took, the spider-ape took sixteen! It was gaining on them fast!

They turned and ran, but they were no match for the spider-ape's eight long legs. It scurried after them like a giant tarantula, using its staff as a crutch for the lame leg. It had almost caught up with them when Carmen spied a break in the rocks ahead. The kids leaped through the crack and plunged into a deep chamber filled with water. The spider-ape crashed against the rocks. It pawed at them with a furry leg, but they were out of its reach.

Carmen and Juni climbed out of the water and into a dark cavern. Shivering, they quickly peeled off their scuba gear and dropped it on the ground. Carmen used Uncle Machete's Elastic Wonder to rub two dry sticks together. Instantly, the sticks caught fire.

"What do you know," said Carmen as she and Juni warmed themselves over the flames. "Thanks, Uncle Machete."

As soon as they were dry, they set out to explore the cave. Not far into the cave, they entered a room filled with golden light. Bright green mold covered the walls and floor.

Gross, Juni thought as he stepped through puddles of slime. *I hate mold.*

Carmen was about to respond . . . when suddenly she realized that Juni's mouth wasn't moving! She looked at him in amazement. *I can hear your thoughts,* she thought.

What? Juni looked at her, puzzled. He'd heard her as clearly as if she had spoken aloud.

And you can hear mine! Say something, she urged him.

Juni opened his mouth to say, "My name is Juni," but no sound came out. He clamped a hand over his mouth in shock. *Aaargh!* he thought.

How strange, Carmen thought. *We can only communicate by thoughts in here.* She looked around the room. *This place is weird. Let's get out of here.*

Juni winked at his sister. *Good idea.*

Carmen and Juni crept further into the cavern. Turning a corner, they abruptly came to a halt. They stared around the room, their mouths hanging open.

Treasure? Juni looked around in wonder. Gold and sparkling jewels spilled from treasure chests in waist-deep piles.

Pirate treasure, Carmen thought back to him. *This area of islands had a lot of pirate traffic back in its day. This must have been where the pirate prisoners were kept.* Juni followed her gaze beyond the treasure to the edge of the room. Skeletons hung from every wall, dangling like strips of bony wallpaper, while the treasure they'd hoarded spilled uselessly at their feet. All the gold in the world hadn't saved these prisoners from their fate. Juni shivered looking at them.

But just as they were about to leave the room, Juni spied a beautiful medallion hanging around a skeleton pirate's neck. He stopped to admire it.

Put it back, Juni! Carmen warned.

Juni rolled his eyes. *I didn't take it yet!*

I can read your mind, remember? Carmen told him. *This land is ancient and cursed. If you take anything, you'll doom us both! Let's go.* Carmen stomped ahead.

Juni hesitated. Then he snatched the medallion, anyway. As he pulled the treasure from its neck, the skeleton clattered to the ground, cracking a hole in its skull. Juni stared at it, then he turned and ran after Carmen.

I think I found the way out, Carmen said, when Juni caught up to her.

Well, hurry up, Juni told her. He glanced nervously back over his shoulder. He could hear strange noises in the tunnel behind them.

But when Carmen climbed into the next room, she found only their scuba gear and their own wet footprints. They'd been going in circles!

We must have made a wrong turn, Carmen said, turning to go back the way they'd come. Juni followed her, anxiously fingering the medallion in his hand. He was starting to feel sorry he'd ever taken it.

Carmen began to jog. Juni could hear her thinking, *I know what we did wrong. We've got to go left.* When they reached the treasure room, Juni stopped. He knelt down to replace the medallion around the skeleton's neck. But the skeleton was gone! Juni frantically scanned the room. Suddenly, he realized the walls were bare. All the skeletons were missing!

Just then he heard a scream. *Oh, no!* Juni thought. *Carmen!*

Juni raced toward the sound of her cry. At the end of a tunnel, the cavern opened out onto a rocky precipice. Carmen stood precariously on its edge, surrounded by a small army of angry skeleton pirates. One skeleton came toward her, waving its sword. With a sweeping kick, she knocked it to the ground. Its bones scattered in every direction. Quickly, Carmen grabbed its sword, shield, and helmet and put them on.

"Juni! Help me!" she cried. With a violent karate chop, Juni shattered the nearest skeleton.

"This shouldn't be too hard," Carmen said, as they faced the mob. "How many do you count now? Twenty-three?"

But she'd spoken too soon. Before their eyes the two fallen pirates magically pulled their shattered bones back together. The other skeletons tossed them new swords. They turned toward Carmen and Juni, ready to fight.

"Twenty-five," Juni said. The skeleton army advanced. Carmen and Juni fought them off, desperately swinging the swords they'd swiped from the fallen pirates. Bones flew through the air, as one by one they knocked the skeletons down. But every time they knocked a skeleton down, the old bones pulled back together and rejoined the fray.

The two kids were starting to get tired. There was no way they could keep up the fight against this magical mob. "We're doomed," Carmen groaned. Suddenly she turned to Juni. "You took something, didn't you?" she said accusingly.

Juni opened his eyes innocently. "No. You told me not to. Why would I?"

Suddenly, a loud screech split the air. Carmen

and Juni looked up. A huge, winged creature was hurtling toward them at a terrifying speed. It snatched Carmen off the ground and flew away with her clutched in its claws.

"Carmen!" Juni cried. Just then, the skeleton with the hole in his head approached him with his bony hand outstretched. Juni dug the medallion out of his pocket and held it out to him.

The skeleton snatched the medallion out of his hand. Then he raised the tip of his sword to Juni's throat. There was no one to save Juni this time. He bravely closed his eyes, resigned to meet his end.

Whoosh! Juni's eyes flew open. The skeleton had whipped his sword around so that the hilt now faced Juni. He was offering Juni his sword. Juni took it, gratefully.

"Thanks, Bones," he said.

As the skeletons marched back to their treasure trove, Juni scrambled over the side of the cliff. He had to find Carmen before something else did!

CHAPTER
18

"Car-men!" Juni shouted for what felt like the hundredth time that afternoon. He'd been searching the jungle for hours, and yet he still hadn't found a single trace of his sister. He was starting to lose hope that he'd ever see her alive again.

Exhausted and discouraged, Juni stepped into a clearing. He looked around. He seemed to have come into some kind of ancient arena. A crumbling stone wall surrounded the area of leveled ground, and a huge carved pillar rose from the center. Juni flopped down on a nearby rock. Digging into his pocket, he pulled out the snack bar.

ROARRRRRRRRR! Juni's head jerked up. The spider-ape emerged from the bushes, howling ferociously. It began to crawl toward him. Juni quickly rewrapped his snack and turned to flee.

To his surprise, the spider-ape's mouth clamped shut! It cocked its head and looked at Juni's food like a puppy begging for a treat. Juni unwrapped the snack again, and the creature growled happily.

"You like honey-roasted ham and potatoes?" Juni asked. "That's what flavor this is. It's highly nutritious. Everything a growing centaur needs." He snapped the bar in two and held out half. The spider-ape snatched the food from his hand and gobbled it down so quickly that Juni was forced to feed him the other half, too. The creature's eyes closed in bliss as he chewed the snack.

Suddenly, a creepy laugh echoed through the arena. Juni spun around. There sat Gary Giggles atop the biggest slizzard Juni had seen!

"Well, well, well," Gary said with a sinister chuckle. "Your friend likes freeze-dry. So does mine." He patted the slizzard's scaly neck. The creature lunged toward Juni, hissing and snapping. Gary tugged its head back with reins he had fashioned from vines, but it was clear to Juni he didn't mean to hold the slizzard back for long. "Can't let you bust up my dad's machine," he said. "So I guess I'll just have to bust *you* up a little."

Juni's face flushed with anger. He took a step toward Gary. But suddenly his path was blocked by a wooden staff. He turned and saw the spider-ape looking at him kindly. It wasn't going to let its new friend fight alone. Grabbing hold of its staff, Juni swung onto the eight-legged creature's back.

Seated astride their monsters, Gary and Juni faced off. The slizzard licked its chops, its slanted eyes rolling wildly in its head. It lunged and almost caught Juni in its fangs. But the spider-ape knocked the huge reptile back with a blow from its powerful legs.

As the two boys battled, the skeleton pirates came rushing into the arena. They tripped over one another, breaking off leg and arm bones in their eagerness to get a good seat. They didn't want to miss the fight!

The skeletons weren't the only ones watching. Hidden in his cave, Romero watched on his miniature island model. "Must try to help them," he gasped. Summoning all his strength, he ran to the door and unlatched it. But when he threw it open, he found a herd of his horrible creatures was waiting there for him. He slammed the door . . . but it fell off its hinges. Oops! Romero's face turned white as the creatures closed in.

But suddenly he found one last ounce of courage. He held up his hands. The creatures stopped in their tracks. "I made *all* of you," he told them. "It's because of me you even exist. So do not eat me."

The creatures paused and looked at him. Romero smiled hopefully. Had they understood him?

ROARRRRRR! With an ear-shattering cry, the creatures closed in. Romero fled from the volcano with a herd of hideous, hungry beasts on his heels.

Meanwhile, Carmen was trapped high atop a cliff in the spork's nest. To her surprise, Gerti was there, too. The spork had snatched her up as well! While the two girls tried to figure out how to escape, Carmen explained what she knew about Donnagon and the Transmooker. But it didn't seem to change Gerti's mind.

"You mean you would still side with your dad over what's right?" Carmen asked.

"Right?" Gerti shrugged. "How do you ever know what's right?"

"When the moment comes, you always know," said Carmen.

Just then, they heard the flap of giant wings and

a loud *screech*. The spork was coming back to its nest! And it sounded hungry!

"I think that moment's come!" Gerti cried.

"Me, too!" Carmen agreed. The two girls leaped from the nest, seconds before the spork swooped in. Carmen and Gerti tumbled through the air. Just before they hit the ground, they opened small parachutes. They landed with a jarring *thud*.

But there was no time to rest. The spork had turned around and was diving toward them again! Carmen and Gerti raced through the jungle. Ahead of them they could hear huge beasts snarling. It sounded like a fight!

Back in the arena, Juni and Gary were in the heat of battle. The slizzard wrapped its snakelike neck around a tall stone pillar. It crashed down onto Juni and the spider-ape! For an instant the spider-ape braced it with its staff, while Juni scrambled away. But it couldn't hold it for long. The heavy pillar toppled onto the creature, pinning one of its legs.

The skeletons stopped cheering and watched silently as the slizzard closed in on Juni. "Ha-hah!" Gary laughed wickedly. "Your creature is lame, and so are you! It's all over for you, squirt. Too bad your dork sister isn't here to cheer me on."

Wham! Suddenly Gary was knocked from the slizzard by something flying through the air. Flat on his back, Gary looked around. To his surprise, he saw Carmen flip off the swinging vine and land gracefully on her feet. She turned to face him with an angry glare. Gary's jaw dropped. He couldn't believe she'd attacked him! And neither could Juni!

The skeletons went wild. One clapped so hard, his hands crumbled into pieces. He picked them up and rattled them like maracas.

But as Carmen stepped toward Gary, the slizzard's serpent head rose up behind her. In a flash, Carmen turned and wrapped her rubber band around the slizzard's mouth, clamping it shut.

"Don't mess with me," she warned, shoving its head away.

Gary picked himself off the ground. "I don't want to hurt you, Carmen," he told her.

Carmen's eyes narrowed. "You are so full of shiitake mushrooms," she snapped. She whipped her hair into a ponytail, ready to rumble.

Gary turned to Gerti for help. But she shook her head. "Don't look at me, brother. You shouldn't fight a girl. You'll lose."

Carmen stepped over to Juni and held out a hand. "I'm siding with you," she told Juni. "But just this once." She smiled.

Juni smiled back and pulled himself to his feet. "Thanks," he said. Grasping each other's hands, they bowed to the audience of cheering skeletons.

But the battle wasn't over yet. The slizzard had snapped free of the rubber band. It reared its neck to strike. Seeing the trouble, the spider-monkey fired a sticky web. The web caught the slizzard and pinned it against the arena wall.

Gary and Gerti grabbed swords from the skeleton pirates, and started to cut the slizzard loose. Carmen and Juni saw their chance to escape.

"We have to destroy the Transmooker device *now*," Carmen said. "Donnagon should be here soon."

"If he's not already," Juni added. Together they leaped onto the spider-ape's back and galloped into the forest.

CHAPTER

19

According to the map Romero had given them, the Transmooker device was in an ancient Aztec temple at the top of a tall, funnel-shaped mountain. Juni and Carmen scaled the mountain and found their way into the heart of the temple. In the center of the ancient room was a large, brightly lit mechanism.

"Is that it?" asked Juni.

"Yes," Carmen answered in a hushed voice.

Juni looked at her. "How do you know?"

"'Cause it's big and weird and in the middle of the room," Carmen said matter-of-factly.

"Good point," Juni said. He walked closer to the device. He could feel the Transmooker's force radiating from the center of the room. When he touched it, his hair stood on end.

"Give me a hand," he said to Carmen. Carmen grabbed it, and her curly brown hair stood up from her head like a halo.

"Careful, Juni," she warned. "If you don't shut it down right, you could bring the entire world as we know it to an abrupt and terrible end."

Juni looked up at her. "Thanks," he said sarcastically.

"I'm serious," said Carmen.

"Well, we have to shut it down." Juni studied the notes Romero had written, then examined the switches on the device.

"This turns that off. That turns this off," he said, flipping two of the switches. Reaching under the machine, he hit two more.

"It says there are five safety switches. But he said there was something tricky about the fifth," Carmen said.

Juni turned to look for the fifth switch, when suddenly the door burst open! Gary and Gerti stood in the doorway.

"Too late, Gary. We got here first," said Juni. "Just stand up against the wall and leave us alone and I won't break every bone in your body."

"Nice try," Gary said. "But we brought friends this time." He stepped aside to reveal Romero.

"Romero!" Juni cried. "What are you doing outside your cave."

"I have no idea," the scientist replied. As he shuffled forward, the kids realized someone was behind him. Just then, Donnagon entered the room, flanked by a team of Magna Men.

"Hello, agents," Donnagon said with a sinister smile. "Warming it up for me?"

This was their last chance to save the world. Juni grabbed the fifth switch and pulled it. But instead of shutting down, the whole machine lit up!

Juni gasped. "What did I do?"

"You started the Transmooker! The world will shut down. Instantly!" Romero cried.

"You said five switches!" Juni looked at him in horror. The room began to shake. Donnagon giggled, his eyes gleaming victoriously.

Suddenly, a huge energy beam burst from the top of the volcano. It fanned out across the sky, shooting in every direction like giant waves of lightning. All across the world, power shut down instantly. From Kansas to Kathmandu, lights, computers, cell phones, cars, trains, and watches all didn't function.

"What do we do?" Juni cried to Romero.

"Bind the five toggle switches together on every side of the podium," Romero told him.

Juni looked at the Transmooker. The switches were far apart—how would he hold them together? Suddenly, he remembered Uncle Machete's Elastic Wonder. Grabbing the rubber band off Carmen's wrist, he stumbled across the shaking floor and quickly wrapped it around five separate switches, pulling them together.

The room stopped shaking. Around the world, lights came back on. The computer screens blinked to life. Everything was back to normal.

As Donnagon and the dazed Magna Men picked themselves up off the floor, Carmen rushed over to the podium. She hit the correct fifth switch, and the Transmooker's main cylinder flew into the air. Quickly, Carmen grabbed it. It was a metal box with a large red button in the center exactly like the prototype the president had held, except it was nearly a foot wide.

Donnagon took a step toward her. "Give it to me," he demanded.

"No," said Carmen. She wasn't about to let Donnagon get his evil hands on the device. But what could she do?

Screeeeech! Carmen glanced at the window and saw the hungry spork swooping through the air outside the temple. Thinking fast, she tossed the cylinder to Romero, who threw it out the window. With a flap of powerful wings, the cylinder disappeared.

"Where did it go?" Donnagon cried, rushing to the window.

"The spork took it!" Romero told him. "Back to its . . ."

"Nest." Carmen looked at Gerti. Gerti looked back at her. They were the only ones who knew where the nest was. Carmen shook her head. "Don't . . ." she warned the younger girl.

But Gerti turned to Donnagon. "I know where the nest is, Dad," she said fiercely.

"Good job, Gerti," he cried. With Gerti leading the way, Donnagon, Gary, and the Magna Men rushed out the door.

"Brat," Carmen snapped as she and Juni hurried after them.

CHAPTER
20

Everyone scrambled down the mountainside, clambering over boulders and slipping down the steep slope. By the time they were halfway down the mountain, Juni, Carmen, and Romero were gasping for air. At this rate, they would never reach the nest before Donnagon and his team.

"Are you sure you know where we're going?" Juni asked.

"My watch has a GPS satellite, you dope. . . ." Carmen started to say. Her sentence trailed off, as it suddenly dawned on her. Her gadgets were working! She turned to Romero. "Can this be?" she asked. Romero nodded.

"When you took out the Transmooker, the island cloaking device was shut down," he told her.

"Well, what are we doing on foot?" she cried. Carmen hit a switch, and her sneakers transformed into rocket shoes. *Whoosh!* She blasted off. With the flick of a switch, Juni rocketed after his sister.

Gary, Gerti, Donnagon, and the Magna Men had almost reached the spork's nest.

"Th . . . there it is!" Gerti gasped, pointing to a mound of straw high on a cliff overhead.

"Okay, Magna Men. We're going to need a human ladder," Donnagon commanded. "One on top of the other, starting right here."

As the Magna Men began to climb atop one another's shoulders, they suddenly heard a strange buzzing sound. They looked up just as Carmen and Juni zoomed overhead. Using her rubber band like a giant sling, Carmen dipped into the nest and scooped up the Transmooker device.

"What?" Gary said in wonder as Carmen flew overhead with the device clutched in her arms.

Carmen smiled and flashed her rubber band at him. "An agent's only as good as her gadgets," she called. Quick as a wink, she and Juni turned and flew off toward the beach.

The instant Carmen and Juni landed on the sand, Carmen hit her remote switch. The bag she'd thrown on the beach earlier that day instantly transformed into a giant tent. Carmen dove inside and began to pull together a number of gadgets.

"What are you doing?" asked Juni.

"Trying to remote-pilot our submarine to the surface so we can get out of here," she replied.

"What can I do?" Juni asked.

"Get on your GPS and see where Mom and Dad are," said Carmen. Juni pulled a small monitor display from his thigh pack and punched in a code to locate their parents.

"This can't be right," Juni said, frowning. "This shows that they are right next to us."

Suddenly, the tent was pulled down around them. Helga and Valentin stood there, their arms open wide for a hug.

"Oh, no!" Juni cried.

"That's no way to greet your grandparents," Helga scolded. Carmen rushed to her and gave her a hug. Valentin floated over to Juni on his hovercraft wheelchair.

"Come here, Juni! Always wear this necklace and I'll always be there," he instructed, hugging the boy tightly.

Juni nodded. "I promise."

Just then, Gregorio and Ingrid rushed up and hugged Carmen tightly, breathing huge sighs of relief.

"Not you guys!" Juni shouted.

Ingrid stared at him. "What's gotten into you?" she asked.

"We thought you might need us!" Gregorio exclaimed.

"I'll always need you, Dad," Juni told him. He began to usher his parents toward the water. "It's great seeing you guys, glad you all could make it. But . . . we need to leave this island, *right now*!"

But it was too late. Donnagon, Gary, and Gerti had arrived on the beach with an army of Magna Men.

"It couldn't be any more perfect," Donnagon said, his lips curling in a sinister smile.

Gregorio stared at Donnagon. Had the leader of the OSS turned on them—again? "This better not be what I think it is," he said.

Donnagon ignored him. "Get the Transmooker device, Felix," he commanded.

The Cortezes gasped. Felix Gumm stepped out from behind a cluster of Magna Men. He grabbed Carmen's bag that held the Transmooker. Ingrid, Gregorio, Helga, and Valentin whipped out their gadgets, ready to attack.

But Donnagon smiled. Slowly he raised his hand. Between his fingers was the small Transmooker prototype he'd taken from the president. He waved it at Ingrid and Gregorio. Instantly, their gadgets shut down.

"A little power goes a long way, doesn't it?" Donnagon chuckled. Standing at his side, Gerti smiled, too. In her hand she held the notebook she'd stolen from Romero's lab.

"Reprogram it, Gerti," Donnagon said, passing the large Transmooker to her. "I want to start by erasing the Cortez family from the face of the earth."

Gerti flipped opened the notebook and scanned through the different formulas. Quickly, she chose one and began to program the code into the Transmooker.

Carmen looked tearfully at Felix. "Uncle Felix, how could you?" she asked.

"I'm not your uncle!" Felix exclaimed. But the corners of his mouth turned down unhappily.

"We treated you like family, Felix. You should be ashamed," said Gregorio.

"Donnagon said if I joined him, he wouldn't get rid of me like he's going to get rid of you," Felix told them.

Donnagon shrugged. "Can't argue with that."

"He knows you'll stop him," Felix added. "So he planned to get you on the island so he could get rid of you *all* at once. And so that no one would avenge you, he sent along your parents."

Helga and Valentin clutched each other in

shock. They had no idea they'd been part of such a sinister plan.

"Donnagon, you're slime," Ingrid growled.

"A good spy always has his eye on the prize," Donnagon told her.

"So I joined him," Felix explained. "I got my daughter to think about, you know."

He looked guiltily at his old friends. "I'm sorry, it won't happen again."

Donnagon chuckled. "Sure won't."

Carmen shifted closer to Juni. "Still have power in your watch?" she whispered out of the side of her mouth.

"Yep."

"Try remote-piloting the choppers," she told him.

Juni smiled just slightly. "Way ahead of you." Using his watch, Juni piloted the choppers so they were hovering in the air behind Donnagon and the Magna Men.

Just then, Gerti handed the device back to Donnagon. "Programming complete, Father."

"Thank you, Gerti," Donnagon said. He pointed the Transmooker at the Cortez family. "Any last words?" he asked.

"Yes," said Ingrid. "But not in front of the children."

"Not to mention your mother," Helga added.

Holding his watch behind his back, Juni continued to steer the choppers so they were right over the Magna Men's heads. Suddenly, the Magna Men began to fly into the air. Their magnetic hats were sticking to the bottom of the choppers! When the last Magna Man had been pulled up, Juni piloted the choppers away, leaving Donnagon, Felix, Gary, and Gerti alone on the beach.

Gregorio faced Donnagon down. "Maybe we could settle this the old-fashioned way," he said. He charged against Donnagon, knocking him into the sand. The Transmooker rolled away as the two men struggled on the ground, fists flying. Their children hovered nearby, calling out advice.

"No, Dad! Take his legs out!" Juni shouted.

"Use his own weight against him!" Gary cried.

"Sleeper hold," cried Carmen.

"Shin kick!" Gerti yelled.

The two men struggled awkwardly in the sand.

"Come on, even I can fight better than that, Gregorio!" Helga called.

Suddenly, Donnagon knocked Gregorio to the

ground with a wild swing. He snatched up the Transmooker and pointed it at Helga and Valentin. But as Donnagon pressed down on the red button, Gregorio leaped in front of his in-laws to shield them from the blast.

Kaboom! The Transmooker instantly exploded in Donnagon's hands. The smoldering pieces crumpled between his fingers and fell to the ground. Everyone stared at them in amazement. What had happened?

Suddenly, Gerti took a cautious step sideways, as if she was trying to sneak away before anyone noticed. Everyone turned to look at her. She had programmed the Transmooker with a self-destruction code! Carmen smiled, and Gerti winked back at her.

"Gerti . . . what did you . . . why?" Donnagon stammered.

"Oh, don't even get me started," she told her father. "Just wait until Mom finds out you tried to take over the world again."

For the first time that day, a look of real fear crossed Donnagon's face. "No! Don't tell your mother! Please!" he cried. Gregorio held his wrists behind his back and dropped him to his knees.

At that moment, the slizzard sneaked up behind Felix and snatched the smaller Transmooker up in its jaws. Felix jumped in fright and whirled around. There sat Romero, riding the slizzard as easily as a cowboy on his horse. His other creatures surrounded him. They were on his side now.

"Gerti," Gary growled, turning to his sister. "You double-crossed your own family."

"I guess I read your spy manual too many times," she snapped back.

Helga and Valentin turned to Gregorio. "You tried to save us," Helga said, her eyes filled with grateful tears. "Why?"

"Because you're my family," Gregorio told her.

Valentin placed a hand on Gregorio's shoulder. "You know, there isn't a man on this planet we'd ever think could be good enough for our daughter, but . . ."

"You come pretty close," Helga finished. Valentin nodded in agreement.

"Blah, blah, blah," Gregorio said, smiling. "I can never understand a word you're saying." He scooped Ingrid into his arms and dipped her backward like a graceful ballroom dancer. She smiled and laughed. As her parents looked on, the happy couple embraced.

Suddenly, the air filled with the beating sound of helicopters. Everyone looked up. An armada of black presidential choppers filled the sky above them like a swarm of giant insects. They touched down on the sand.

The president stepped out of the largest chopper and looked around. To Juni's surprise, Alexandra stepped out behind him. The president whispered something in her ear. She nodded, then turned and walked over to Gary. Taking hold of his Level One badge, she removed it from his neck.

"By order of the president, you've been temporarily disavowed," she told him. She turned to Donnagon. "You're fired," she said. Then she walked over to Gregorio, "And so, by order of the president, you are the new director of the OSS."

Gregorio glanced at Ingrid's parents. Valentin nodded and raised his eyebrows. He was impressed.

Alexandra handed Gary's Level One badge to Juni. Juni grinned and flashed the badge triumphantly at Gary.

Gary scowled and slipped a pair of sunglasses over his eyes. "I guess I lost this round," he said, his lips curling angrily. "But I'll be back."

"I hope you're on the good side next time," said Carmen.

"We'll see, but . . ."—Gary paused as the polarized lenses of his glasses darkened, blocking out his eyes—"you never know." Two government officials came up and took him by the arm.

As they led him away, Gerti turned to Carmen. "Don't worry," she said. "If he gets out of line, I'll straighten him out."

Carmen grinned. "Go, Gerti," she cheered.

Meanwhile, Juni had handed the Level One badge back to Alexandra. She looked at him in surprise. "You don't want it?"

He shook his head. "I'm leaving the OSS," he explained. "I've seen what it takes to be a top spy. And I think I can be of better use to the world by just being the best . . . me."

"What about all the cool gadgets?" Alexandra asked.

"Got the best one right here." Juni said, holding up the rubber band. He snapped it to her. She caught it and placed it around her wrist like a bracelet. They smiled at each other.

"See you around?" asked Juni.

"Yes," said Alexandra.

It was time to go home. Juni and Carmen watched as their parents and grandparents climbed into one of the presidential choppers.

Well . . . go ahead. Say it. Carmen spoke to Juni with her thoughts, just as she had when they were in the treasure room.

What? he asked.

Carmen rolled her eyes. *I told you so.*

Juni looked at his sister and grinned. *Never.*

They climbed into the chopper with their parents and fastened their seat belts. But just as they were about to lift off, Romero came rushing toward them across the sand. "Wait! Wait!" he cried. He reached into the chopper and handed Juni a box.

"Thank you," said Juni. He looked past Romero and saw the spider-ape, the slizzard, a spork . . . all Romero's creatures had come to the beach to say good-bye. Even a few of the skeleton pirates stood in the sand, waving.

Juni grinned. "You got it, boss," he said. As the chopper rose into the air, he felt a lump in his throat. He would miss his spider-ape friend. He pressed his face against the window glass and waved until he couldn't see his pal anymore.

Suddenly, the box in Juni's lap began to shake. He opened it up. Out crawled the miniature spider-ape! It climbed onto Juni's shoulder. To Juni's delight, it began to roar and beat its chest. At the same time, the full-sized spider-ape stood on the sandy beach hundreds of feet below, roaring and beating his chest in sync with the miniature version. As the helicopter sailed into the clouds, Juni smiled to himself, knowing he would never forget his adventure on Leeke Leeke Island.

Down below on the beach, Romero waved until the chopper containing the Cortez family was just a speck in the sky. Suddenly, he saw something out of the corner of his eye. He turned. A small boat pulled up to the beach. Out stepped a large man with a white-toothed grin.

"Well, well, well, well, well," said Dinky Winks, wading toward the startled scientist. "You're not an easy man to find. You and your Leeke Leeke Island." He whipped a business card out of his pocket and handed it to Romero. "I'm Dinky . . . Winks, that is."

Romero studied the business card, perplexed.

Dinky eyed the slizzard, the spider-ape, and all Romero's other strange creatures. "Heard you had a wild place here. Thought you'd be interested in a proposition. You ready?" He grinned and held out his arms wide. "Theme park!" he exclaimed. "Think about it. Families on safari. Crazy creatures running around."

The slizzard sniffed at Dinky. Dinky stretched out a hand to pet it. *Snap!* The slizzard bit down on his hand. Dinky grimaced and clutched his hand. It looked like his fingers were gone! Romero gasped.

But it was just a Dinky trick. Dinky lifted his hand and wiggled his fingers, which he'd been hiding behind his hand. Romero sighed in relief.

"Ha-ha-ha," Dinky chuckled. "You can see it already, can't you?" He placed an arm around Romero's shoulder. "We'll be great together."